BLACKSTONE RANGER GUARDIAN

Blackstone Rangers Book 5

ALICIA MONTGOMERY

Also by Alicia Montgomery

THE TRUE MATES SERIES

Fated Mates

Blood Moon

Romancing the Alpha

Witch's Mate

Taming the Beast

Tempted by the Wolf

THE LONE WOLF DEFENDERS SERIES

Killian's Secret

Loving Quinn

All for Connor

THE TRUE MATES STANDALONE NOVELS

Holly Jolly Lycan Christmas

A Mate for Jackson: Bad Alpha Dads

TRUE MATES GENERATIONS

A Twist of Fate

Claiming the Alpha

Alpha Ascending

A Witch in Time

Highland Wolf

Daughter of the Dragon

Shadow Wolf

A Touch of Magic

Heart of the Wolf

THE BLACKSTONE MOUNTAIN SERIES

The Blackstone Dragon Heir

The Blackstone Bad Dragon

The Blackstone Bear

The Blackstone Wolf

The Blackstone Lion

The Blackstone She-Wolf

The Blackstone She-Bear

The Blackstone She-Dragon

BLACKSTONE RANGERS SERIES

Blackstone Ranger Chief

Blackstone Ranger Charmer

Blackstone Ranger Hero

Blackstone Ranger Rogue

Blackstone Ranger Guardian

Blackstone Ranger Scrooge

COPYRIGHT © 2020 ALICIA MONTGOMERY
WWW.ALICIAMONTGOMERYAUTHOR.COM
FIRST ELECTRONIC PUBLICATION NOVEMBER 2020

EDITED BY LaVERNE CLARK
COVER BY JACQUELINE SWEET
111720

Chapter 1
A FEW MONTHS AGO ...

The humongous grizzly bear trudged through the blanket of snow on the ground, unbothered by neither the dangerously low temperatures nor the fast falling flakes piling up on its large block head and burly body. It continued to lumber along through the trees, going farther up the mountain.

Up here, John Krieger allowed his animal to take over their shared body. With the bear in charge, their senses remained sharp, their body could hold up against the elements, while the human side remained dull and suppressed.

It was the only place safe enough to allow the beast its freedom.

A howl in the distance made the bear pause. Krieger recognized the sound, as did his bear. *Milos.* He was their nearest neighbor—if he could be called that. He had never seen the wolf shifter in human skin, but Damon had told him about the other man's presence on the mountain when he arrived about a year ago. Since then, the two of them had encountered each other a handful of times, both in animal form. While many in the past would have turned tail and run, the one-eyed wolf showed no fear in the presence of the mighty grizzly. In fact, Krieger had not sensed much of anything at all in the other shifter, except maybe recognizing their sameness. Here was another broken animal, hiding out from the world.

A few heartbeats passed, and there was no more howling. Was it a warning? Of what? Up here, near the highest peaks of the Blackstone Mountains, there were no dangers, at least not to apex predators like them. There was hardly anything or anyone up here at all, not in the dead of winter. The real bears were all deep in their den, hibernating. Perhaps there might be an odd shifter or two, but that was rare in this weather.

The grizzly continued on. They had a job to do, after all, and Krieger took his work as a Blackstone Ranger seriously, guarding the entrance to Contessa Peak for the last five years. There were a few hikers who dared scale the peak in better weather, so he always made sure they made it up and back down safely.

Mostly, though, it was shifters who roamed up here. After all, this was a sanctuary for all of their kind who lived in Blackstone, the one place they could truly feel safe in their animal skins. It was his job, too, to protect them and make sure they remained undisturbed.

Of course, there were the shifters that didn't need protection, that is, they were the ones who protected the entirety of Blackstone itself. The Lennoxes were a family of dragons—four in total—who owned the mountains and the minerals in them that had made them one of the richest families in the world. Though Krieger had never met any of them personally, he'd seen them several times in the last few years, flying and dipping like gigantic graceful butterflies as they chased each other or conducted flying races, using the jagged crown of Contessa Peak as a finish line. The largest one was the sire, and then there were the twin males who were indistinguishable from each other, and the smaller female one, who seemed just as fierce as her brothers.

Yes, he took this job seriously. It was not only his life, but also his salvation, allowing him to live and remain undisturbed for the most part. Encounters with others were few and far between, he made sure of that. He used his excellent sense of hearing and smell to keep track of who and what was up and around Contessa Peak. If he found a lost hiker or shifter, it was easy enough to call HQ to have them picked up or rescued, watching over them until help came. Rarely did he come near others. No, it was too much. Too risky.

He continued on, rounding the perimeter of his patrol area. All rangers on duty had a schedule and a route to follow, but his sole area of responsibility remained the same. It didn't matter what day or time it was. There was a sheet of paper tacked up in his cabin with his hours and days of duty, but it had been so faded, he could barely read the print. For him, there were no weekends, no vacations, no off-hours. Contessa Peak was his responsibility, his to protect at all hours, all days. The patrol, the job, the guard, that was all that mattered to him and his bear. They were entrusted by the chief and the Blackstone Dragons to keep everyone here safe, and so that's what they would do. He was very good at following orders, after all.

The wind, which had already been whipping when he left his little cabin, had now picked up. As the minutes and hours passed, it grew stronger, blowing sleet across the mountains. *Not good*, Krieger thought. A freak snowstorm, perhaps.

The CB radio he had in his cabin was the only form of communication he had to the outside world. He relied on it for information, from which ranger worked what area to alerts for lost hikers, but more important, weather for the day. The dispatcher hadn't said anything about a storm coming this morning, so it must have blown in from out of nowhere.

Need to turn back, he told his bear. Sure, if things got rough, they could probably dig a den in the ground and hold up until it passed, but why bother when he knew exactly where they were and how far the walk back to the cabin was? Despite the nearly white-out conditions, his keen sense of direction was like a compass, keeping him oriented at all times.

The bear lumbered around, but halted halfway. *What the hell—*

There.

His grizzly picked up on it before he did. The sound was faint, but it was there.

Small, slowing faint footsteps of four paws trudging through snow.

A pathetic scritch-scratch sound.

A heartbeat.

Someone was out there. And they were in trouble.

Bear and man were one in body and mind as they focused their senses. Nearby, for sure. The bear followed the sounds, like a beacon in the white vastness of the storm. The footsteps had stopped now. Then the little panting sounds. Until finally it was just the patter of the heartbeat, slowing down to a near halt.

Six feet to the left, about two feet below the snow.

How he and his bear knew where the sounds came from, Krieger didn't question. There was only the need to find out whatever it was and help them. The layer of snow was no match for the bear's paws as it dug through the ice like it was paper. Finally, buried underneath all that white, bits of red fur began to appear. Krieger had to slow his animal down, directing its sharp claws to dig around the poor, half-frozen creature, and pull it out.

Huh.

It was so small in his giant paws, but it was obvious now what it was, from the reddish and gray fur, pointed snout and ears, plus the black-tipped paws. A fox. Its bushy red tail hung down, limp, like the rest of its body.

Poor thing. Its ragged breaths and faintly beating heart told him the creature was still alive, but just barely. *Shifter,* his animal instinct whispered.

His bear roared loudly, a garbled sound his ears couldn't decipher. It was as if it was trying to catch his attention, telling him something.

Need to get out of the cold. Get it warm and dry in the cabin. He usually avoided dealing directly with hikers and other shifters, but there was no time to contact HQ, nor would he leave this creature out in the cold to freeze to death. Carefully tucking it into the crook of its arm, the bear got onto two feet and began the long walk back to their den.

The fox didn't stir or make any more sounds in their arms. *Out cold.* Shifters were stronger than their human or animal counterparts, but they still had their limits. Maybe this little creature overestimated theirs or it, too, had been caught in the sudden storm. He could imagine that it got lost, then turned around when the storm came in.

Finally, he spied the light of his cabin in the distance. By now, the storm was in full force, and if he didn't have his sense of direction or keen senses, he would have been lost too. His strength, though, had dwindled from all that work, so he shifted back as he trudged up the porch steps, now fully human as his hand reached for the doorknob and staggered inside.

The lights flickered overhead before dying, plunging the cabin into darkness. *Got here just in time, thank fuck.*

He was bone-tired, but he still had his little friend to think about. The fox remained tucked into the crook of his arm. It looked bigger than he initially thought, a full-grown adult, he reckoned. Still, it didn't move. The breathing was more even now, but its body remained heavy, perhaps conserving its energy to heal itself. He could relate—he, too, was exhausted. So, he stumbled toward the largest piece of furniture in the single living space in his cabin—the bed—and collapsed on top of it. As his eyelids grew heavier and heavier, he tucked the fox closer to his body, sharing his warmth, then passed out cold, but not before he made out what his bear had been trying to say.

Mine.

Chapter 2

Cold. *Freezing cold.*

That was the last thing Dutchy Forrester felt before her poor fox's body gave out from fatigue.

The snowstorm appeared out of nowhere and whirled around them, making them lose their sense of direction. Up was down and down was up. As a shifter, she should have been able to last through hours of physical activity, but between trying to keep their body warm and trudging through piling snow, they had depleted their energy stores until it simply ran out.

Should have known my limits. But the call of the mountains and fresh air and trees was too much, and she'd been working her human side hard these past months. After all, her business had finally gotten off the ground and reaching heights she never thought possible.

However, eighty-hour weeks doing nothing but designing, sewing, fitting, and dealing with clients were taking its toll, and her fox finally said, *enough.* It wanted to get out, be in nature. And so, she let it free and let it roam, in one of the safest places she knew—up in the Blackstone Mountains where others like her could just be themselves.

The fox had been elated. After weeks and weeks of being trapped, it was finally free. Free to run and roll around in the dirt and dig with claws and hunt tiny prey. Dutchy couldn't bear to pull it back; besides, being in animal form for a few hours always gave her the best burst of creative energy. In fox form, her senses were stronger—smells so much more pungent, sounds so clear even from a distance.

And the colors. Oh, the colors! Even in the winter, they were beautiful. The pure verdant of the pine trees. Deep browns of tree bark. Rich, black soil under their paws. And the bright blue sky ... there was nothing in her collection of colored pencils and markers that could do justice to such an indescribable color. Ideas bloomed in her head as her creative energy flourished.

She'd been so wrapped up in the throes of inspiration that she hadn't noticed the sky turning gray or the wind picking up. By the time she saw the snow whipping around them, it had been too late. She had no idea where her fox had taken her. Everything was white and cold.

Was she dead? The afterlife seemed terribly dark. And lumpy. At least it was underneath her. Everywhere else, it was warm. No, it was *hot*.

Uh-oh. Maybe I ended up in the other *place.*

The heat seemed to be concentrated behind her, as something hard pressed along the backside of her body. She found she could wiggle her toes and fingers, but the rest of her limbs were immobilized, held together by vise-like devices.

What the hell?

As her brain's function slowly returned, her shifter vision adjusted to the darkness. She wasn't in some kind of purgatory waiting room. Unless purgatory was a log cabin and a lumpy mattress. And those vises keeping her immobile? Those were definitely arms. Large, muscled, hairy arms. Belonging to a large, muscled, hairy *male*.

Oh God.

Her entire body froze. Her brain went on alert. *Danger.* However, her fox didn't make a move or a sound. Normally, it would warn her, kicking in her flight or fight instinct. But no, her animal remained docile. Curious, even.

Stop messing around, she told it. They had to get out of here. Who knows what this man was capable of?

A warm breath blew on her neck, a tingle traveled up her body, from her toes to the top of her head.

Oooohhhh.

A hot, embarrassing flush of arousal coursed through her. What the hell? Was it too early to have Stockholm Syndrome?

Okay, she told her fox. *If I shift, that would make us small enough to escape these tree trunks he has for arms. Then we can run—*

But the fox shook its head and hunkered down, as if to say, *nuh-uh, no way.*

Are you crazy? She mentally pulled her hair out. We can't—

The hulking male's grip loosened, and her brain told her to go. *Now.* With a deep breath, she planted an elbow on the mattress and pushed herself off the bed. She hadn't even moved an inch before she landed flat on her back, the very hard—and very naked—male body pinning her down.

The urge to fight was there, but somehow, her body didn't work. No, instead, she looked up at her captor, her gaze colliding with bright blue eyes.

Oh.

Forget about the blue winter sky. No, these eyes were the *true* indescribable blue.

Mine.

Was that—

Mine, the voice inside her repeated.

And a deep, beautifully haunting sound from somewhere deep in him replied. *Mine.*

"You're my—"

She never finished the sentence as his mouth crashed over hers. The kiss was savage, with an edge of hunger she'd never felt before, from anyone or herself. It was consuming and at the same time, she wanted to devour him too. The taste of him was incredible—smoky, rich, and oh so male. And his scent. She wanted it all over herself, wanted to drown in it until she died a blissful, happy death.

Large hands cupped the sides of her face. They were rough and calloused, and when he shoved his fingers into her scalp and tugged, a zing of pleasure went straight to her core. He must have smelled her arousal because he huffed in response. One of his hands grazed down her body, leaving a hot trail over her skin. He spread her knees, his fingers going straight to the sweet spot between her thighs.

She moaned into his mouth as the pads of his rough fingertips caressed her wet outer lips. His touch was surprisingly gentle, moving up and down tentatively before delving into her. Her hips bucked off the mattress, wanting more. Wanting it all.

He rewarded her with a nip to her lips and pushing another finger inside her.

"Oh!" she gasped when he pulled his mouth away from her. His lips grazed lower, licking a path down her neck, all the way to her breasts. Her nipples were now painfully hard nubs, and she let out another moan when his wet, hot mouth covered one.

Between the lashing of his tongue on her nipples and his fingers playing her expertly, her body exploded in an orgasm, her brain short-circuiting from the mindless pleasure.

Her body was still recovering when he pushed her thighs

apart and moved between them. *This was really happening.* And, God help her, she wanted it.

He loomed above her, and she found herself drawn up to those eyes again. They stared down at her, like blazing twin orbs of blue fire, reaching deep into her, all over, until there was no part of her that remained untouched.

Mine. Mine. Mine, her soul repeated, pulsing to the beat of her heart. Something blunt and large pushed at her wet entrance, slowly pushing inside her. When she winced at his girth, he stopped. But despite her body's protest, she wanted him to continue.

With a deep breath, she nudged her hips up at him. She could sense his hesitation.

"Please," she breathed. "I need you."

His answer of a soft growl sent out a ripple of pleasure across her skin. He inched inside her, slowly, allowing her to accommodate him in her narrow passage. When he was fully seated in her, she relaxed her muscles.

His mouth descended on hers again, capturing hers in another hungry kiss. His hips began to move, and the friction of him inside her made her body spasm. She clung to him, her arms going up to his shoulders, her fingers raking down his muscled back. He let out a guttural sound and pounded into her faster.

Needy, desperate moans and cries escaped her mouth, and she found herself meeting his thrusts. Hands and lips moved everywhere, kissing and touching every bit of skin. Her legs wrapped around his trim waist, heels digging into his buttocks as she urged him on. Faster. Harder. It was as if he was reading her mind, so in tune with her body that he knew what she needed.

Their lips met again, her mouth opening up to him as he devoured her. Her body went taut, his hands pushed under her, lifting her up at just the right angle to send her into the stratosphere with a mind-blowing orgasm that made her vision go white. He grunted, a low, primal sound that seemed to stretch out as his body shuddered with his own pleasure. His cock pulsed inside her, and she milked him, wanting every last drop of him. Instead of slowing down, he moved faster, gripping her ass so hard he probably bruised it. The pleasure–pain was enough to wring another orgasm from her before they both collapsed.

As her breathing returned to normal and her heartbeat slowed, the first thing she thought was, *I don't even know this man.*

Yes, you do, a voice said from inside her. *He's your mate.*

In all honesty, Dutchy never thought she had a mate or that she'd even meet hers. It seemed all her friends in Blackstone had found the other half of their souls, except for her. It wasn't that she was desperate to find her mate, but she'd seen how happy her friends were, had even designed and made all their wedding dresses, so she asked herself, *why can't I have that?*

The irony that he was here in Blackstone all this time wasn't lost on her.

All right, so he's my mate. But who is he?

A mumbling jolted her out of her thoughts—though she wasn't likely to forget she was still pinned under the hulk of a man who gave her three mind-blowing orgasms and was still inside her. But she was afraid to open her eyes. Afraid that if she did, he might disappear.

The weight on top of her lifted up, and she sucked in a breath as he withdrew from her. He rolled over, the mattress dipping as he settled beside her. To her surprise, an arm snaked around to pull her to his chest.

Oh. Her mate was a cuddler. That seemed ... sweet. She snuggled up to him, enjoying his warmth and scent, nuzzling at his hairy chest. His body was like a big heater, so she didn't need a blanket.

From the steady rise and fall of his chest, he must have fallen asleep. Despite the burning curiosity, she tamped down the urge to look up at him. Instead she glanced around her, at least, what she could see from this angle.

The trace scent of pine told her they were in some kind of log cabin. There was an old-fashioned stove in the corner, which meant this was probably the only room. The walls were bare, but who needed decor when the large windows had views of the outside anyway—at least, they probably did, but she couldn't tell because it was dark.

The temptation to look up at him and study his face grew stronger, but she resisted again. She was too embarrassed. *I mean, who has sex with the complete stranger they woke up with?*

Well, technically he wasn't a stranger, she reminded herself. It was difficult to describe, only that she was drawn to him. It was probably too soon for the bond to form, at least from what her friends told her. Sybil—or rather, Queen Sybil now—told her that according to her husband, it would only form when both parties were ready and open to accepting it. Sometimes it happened in a few days, other times in a few months. It could even be broken and fixed again. It was scary—and exciting—to wonder how her story would play out, like in all those romance novels she loved to read whenever she had the time.

When his breathing evened out, she extricated herself from his arms and slipped out of bed. The delicious pain between her legs made her wince, but also shiver in delight. When was the last time she came that hard? Too long.

Gingerly, she tiptoed to the door she assumed was the bathroom and pushed inside. Thankfully, it was the bathroom, and she did her business and wiped herself down with a towel hanging on the rack. As she put herself in some order of semblance, she glanced around. The bathroom was bare, but serviceable. There were no personal items anywhere, except a toothbrush, a tube of toothpaste, and soap. A uniform shirt hanging on the back of the door caught her eye.

"Blackstone Rangers," she whispered, reading the logo above the left-hand pocket. Unable to stop herself, she pressed the khaki fabric to her nose and took a whiff. *Oh.* It smelled so good. Smelled like *him*. The urge to wrap it around herself was strong, so she took it off the hook and slipped it on, wrapping it around her like a robe. The shirt was huge, of course, as she was already short at five foot three, but he must be huge because the thing hung down past her knees. *Maybe I'll get to see him vertical at some point,* she mused.

Carefully tiptoeing out, she crept back toward the bed. The sight of him made her halt. *Oh my.*

He was magnificent. His large, naked body sprawled out over the bed; long hair spread on the pillows. Broad muscled shoulders, arms dotted with tattoos. Perfectly-formed chest covered with a dark mat of hair extending down over an impressive set of eight-pack abs. His cock—oh dear—even flaccid it was intimidating, and she now knew why she would be walking funny for a while.

Stop drooling, she told herself. They'd already had sex, so she shouldn't be acting like some hormonal teenager. With a shake of her head, she crept back into bed, keeping an eye on him in case he woke up. Thankfully, his eyes remained closed, though she was longing to see those blue orbs again. A shiver went through her as she lay down next to him, but not touching him. She tucked her legs under the humungous shirt. She wasn't sleepy, but she closed her eyes anyway until her body relaxed and she drifted off, surrounded by the warmth of his shirt and his intoxicating scent.

Light filled the room when Dutchy woke up, but that wasn't why her eyes flew open.

No, it was the weight of the hot, hard body on top of her.

Shock coursed through her as her gaze moved downwards, her gaze colliding with blue eyes. The two blazing orbs pinned her as he pulled the shirt she wore open and took a nipple between his lips.

"Nnngghh!" Her fingers dug into his scalp, tugging at the hair, as if she could get him closer. His response was to take as much of her breast into his mouth and graze the sensitive tip with his teeth.

She moaned again, bucking her hips up. When his knees nudged her thighs apart, she braced herself to receive him, but to her surprise, he released her breast, and crawled lower.

Her eyes practically rolled to the back of her head when his mouth touched her slick lips. Her fingers fisted into the sheets as her body tensed from the growing pressure building in her. A growl startled her, making her head snap down.

He was staring at her as he devoured and licked at her. The noises rang through the quiet cabin filling it with filthy, depraved sounds that only fueled her desire. Though her cheeks flushed with embarrassment at how much he was enjoying himself, she couldn't turn away. When her lids started to close, he only growled louder and sped up the motion of his mouth.

As his lips found her clit, he had to hold her down to keep her hips on the mattress. When he sucked back hard, she let go, letting the orgasm ripple through her body.

She was barely coming down when he flipped her to her stomach, pushed the shirt up, and kicked her knees apart. Covering her back with his body, he surged into her in one motion.

"Oh God!" She clung to the sheets, her buttocks lifting back to meet his thrusts. At this angle, his cock stroked the most sensitive places in her. One hand thrust into her scalp, fingers tangling in her hair. When he pulled back, she nearly howled as a wave of pleasure wracked her body.

He hauled her up to her hands and knees, and she braced herself against his powerful hips as he rutted into her. A hand shoved between her legs and his fingers plucked at her clit, coaxing another orgasm from her body.

She thought she was truly wrung out by then, but he was relentless. His hands grabbed at her shoulder and pulled her up to him, a hand wrapping around her breast to play with her nipple, while the other pushed her hair aside so his mouth could suck at the sensitive skin on her neck.

"Please!" As his teeth nipped at her shoulder, her body shook with pleasure.

He half growled–grunted against her, his cock twitching as he emptied into her, flooding her insides with his warm seed. His thrusts slowed, his grip around her tightened, and he twisted her head around to catch her mouth in a hot, sensuous kiss.

When he released her, she sighed and fell back down on the bed, his cock slipping out of her. As she felt the mattress dip and rise as he left the bed, she closed her eyes.

She must have dozed off, because her body felt stiff when she opened her eyes again, like she'd been in the same position for hours. Though there were trace scents of him, she knew he wasn't in the bed. The feeling of being alone unnerved her, and she quickly sat up.

"You're awake."

The low, rough timbre of the voice sent warmth through her. Her head snapped toward the source—it was him, of course. He stood by the stove, bare-chested, arms crossed over his chest.

His jeans hung low on his hips; top buttons opened. Blue eyes peered right at her, pinning her until a hot, furious blush crept up her neck.

"Um, yeah." Realizing she was still wearing his shirt—which was parted and showed a generous amount of her breasts—she grabbed the lapels and pulled them shut. "Sorry. I didn't have anything else to wear." They'd already had sex twice at this point, why the heck was she so embarrassed?

He gave a noncommittal grunt. "I have food. And coffee." He cocked his head at the table in front of him.

Now that intrigued her. And her hungry stomach. Scrambling off the bed, she padded toward the kitchen–dining area. As she drew nearer, her fox came to life, sparked by his presence. The animal yipped excitedly, as if reminding her who this man was to them.

Not that she was likely to forget.

"Thanks," she murmured as she sat on the lone chair. The coffee smelled great, and there was toast and a heap of eggs and bacon. "Have you—"

The light flickered overhead.

"I should check on the panels." Without another word, he brushed past her and headed out the door, into the cold and snow.

Reaching for a piece of toast, she nibbled at the end. Did he regret sleeping with her? But they were mates. Okay, so maybe they should have gotten a few things out of the way first—like each other's names—but the instinct was too strong. It was difficult to deny she wanted him as much as he did. Initially anyway. His gruff manner unnerved her, but maybe that's just the way he was.

Her fox wagged its bushy tail, agreeing with her.

Yeah, that's it. It was obvious the sassy little creature was infatuated with their mate.

What was he anyway? Something large, for sure. She had sensed his animal, of course, but only fleetingly.

Minutes ticked by, and he didn't come back. So, she ate some more toast, eggs, and a couple of pieces of bacon and washed it down with the cooling coffee. When she was full, she put the food away and brought the dirty dishes to the sink.

A quick glance out the window as she cleaned up the dishes told her the worst of the storm had passed, but everything was covered in a thick blanket of snow. How bad was the storm? And where the heck was she, anyway? How would she get back home, and what was going to happen now?

The door slamming against the wall shook her out of her thoughts. He stood in the doorway, completely naked, jeans in one hand, shaking the flakes that had clung to his beard and hair. It was obvious he had shifted to his animal form while outside.

A thrill ran down her spine, and her fox *scritched* with excitement. There it was, his animal. Fierce and strong and wild. It called to her. Tugged at her, and her instincts told her to reach out and—

The animal pulled back, as if he had reined it in and locked it away. The move made her start, as did the flash of anger in his eyes.

Turning away, she attempted to concentrate on washing the dishes, though she could hear every move he made, from the moment he closed the door to when he shucked on his jeans and walked up behind her. She tensed, sensing him inches away.

"My name is Duchess Forrester, by the way," she began as she dried her plate. Maybe it was better not to look at him, because those indescribable blue eyes had only one effect on her. "But most people call me Dutchy."

A heartbeat passed. "John. I'm John Krieger."

John Krieger. My mate's name is John Krieger. "Um, nice to meet you, John." She remained with her back to him, and she told herself it was because she still had to dry the rest of the dishes.

"I'm sorry. About ..."

Her hands stilled as his palms hovered over her shoulders. When they landed lightly, she said, "Don't."

He pulled them away as if he'd been burned.

Sensing his recoil, she quickly placed the plate back into the sink and whirled around. "No." She placed her hands on his chest. Muscles jumped under her touch, and he sucked in a breath. "I mean, don't be sorry. About what happened between us. I wanted it." She lifted her head to meet his eyes, the blue gaze sucking her in like a black hole she couldn't pull free from. "I still want it. Want you."

His mouth came down so quick and hard on hers, she barely had time to take in a breath. His lips drank from hers hungrily, and she found herself being lifted up, her legs wrapping around his waist. She thought he was going to bring her back to bed, but instead, he planted her on the table, pushing his jeans down to take out his already engorged cock.

"Ohh." She braced herself as he moved between her thighs. The tip of his cock teased at her clit, making her body shudder with little shocks of pleasure. "Please, John." An arm came around her as he pushed into her, filling her with the familiar feeling of him.

He held her close, kissing and touching every bit of skin he could reach. Her arms, too, wound around him, clinging to him desperately as their bodies raced to the finish line, both of them shaking as they each reached the heights of their pleasure.

When it was all over, she plastered herself against his chest, afraid to let go lest she melted into a puddle on the floor. He lifted her up, cradled her close and carried her to the bed. He attempted to pry her away, but she clung to him tighter. So, he lay them on top of the mattress, cuddling her close as she nuzzled at his side.

Silence stretched on until she cleared her throat. "Um, John. I wanted to ask ... where are we?" Her hand played over his chest, enjoying the feel of the rough hair under her fingertips.

"Ranger Cabin. Just outside the entrance to Contessa Peak." His voice had a rough-hewn quality, as if those were the most words he'd spoken aloud in a long time.

"Contessa Peak?" That was really far away from where she'd started. *How did you get all the way up here?* she asked her fox. The little creature only shrugged.

"You didn't know?"

She shook her head and told him what she did remember. "... and uh, then I woke up here."

He grunted. "Found you while patrolling in the snow. Your fox was half frozen. Brought you back."

"Patrolling?" *Oh right.* He was one of the Blackstone Rangers. She didn't know much about them, only that they protected the areas around the mountains, much like park rangers in national forests and parks. "The storm. It came out of nowhere."

A sound rumbled from his chest. "Yeah."

Good thing this ranger cabin was here. Probably had it for emergencies like this. "So ... when do you think we'll get back?"

"Back?"

"Back home. To town."

There was a pause. "Half the solar panels were knocked out. Should have enough power for two days if we conserve the batteries. I'll start up the radio and call into HQ. Roads are probably out for now. Might be a while before they can send transport in the morning."

She glanced outside again. The snow was still falling,

though it was calmer now. A million questions zinged through her head. Who was this man, her mate? What did he do for fun? Where did he live? And of course, what would happen when they got back?

Her fox wrinkled its nose at her, as if to say, *stop*. Just enjoy the moment. They were mates, there would be time enough for that.

And so, putting those thoughts aside, she snuggled deeper against his side.

Chapter 3

His mate.

The words rang in Krieger's head over and over again, the synapses unable to make the connection, even as he held her in his arms.

His bear growled in protest.

No!

He reined the creature in. It could not touch her. Not his perfect, gorgeous mate. His hand swept down the skin of her naked back, milky white and unmarred except for a smattering of freckles on her shoulders. The imperfection only made her more appealing to him, though, and he found his eyes tracing the little dots.

She shifted around, her coppery red hair spilling over his arm. *Christ.* Redheads had always been his weakness. Once upon a time. Different lifetime. Different man.

Certain parts of that life remained in his brain. Teasing. Kissing. Fucking. The skills to please a woman and have her begging for more. But with her ... it was different. All those before her melted away from his memories.

A mate. God, he didn't deserve her.

The grizzly rose again, and he shut it away, ignoring its protests. He was more forceful this time. *Have to keep it locked up. Can't have her see. Have her tainted.*

His past would remain in the past. Up here, it was easy to forget. A sheen of cold sweat built up on his forehead.

The dampness of the market basement.

Shuffle of boots behind him.

His eardrums bursting from the boom.

Rubble around him.

Cries.

Blood.

Hours. Days. Slowly dehydrating. Dying.

And then the horrors of what happened after.

A strangled cry fought to escape his throat, and he wrestled it down.

"John? John?"

Deep breaths. Deep breaths. He focused on the beautiful face looking up at him, sparkling pale blue eyes the color of robin's eggs bringing him back to now. *Duchess Forrester.* His mate.

"Are you all right?" She reached up to caress his cheek.

He nuzzled at her soft palm. "Am now."

"You seemed far away."

Very far. Halfway around the world, in another life.

He cleared his throat. "Are you hungry?" Hours had passed since their last meal. After breakfast—which had been closer to lunchtime—and their nap, he woke her up again for another round of fucking. After feasting on her sweet little pussy, he hauled her up, and she rode him until they were both panting from earth-shaking orgasms. Jesus, he didn't need food—he could eat her all day.

"I put breakfast away," she said with a delicate yawn. "We

can heat it up." She stretched her arms over her head and sat up, pulling his shirt around her body.

Though he didn't like that she covered up those lovely large tits, he did like seeing his clothes on her. The name on the right side of the uniform shirt had faded away long ago, but the idea of having his mark on her like that made him rumble in pleasure. That and his *other* marks on her, especially the traces of him between her legs.

"I'd really like a shower." Her pert little nose wrinkled. "I'm sure I could use one."

He shook his head, then pulled her down to him, making her squeal in surprise. "You smell fine." Pressing his nose to the side of her neck, he inhaled. She smelled like him. He liked that. Having her wash it away did not please him.

She laughed. "John, seriously. I haven't taken a bath in over a day. I love bubble baths, and I could spend hours in one, but we probably don't have that luxury up here. Is there enough power for a hot shower? Even for just a minute. I don't want to use up what we have left."

His mate seemed really keen on a shower, and he supposed she was used to luxuries like unlimited hot water. "It's fine. Use what you want." A thousand cold showers would be worth it to make her feel more at home here.

She rewarded him with a kiss to the nose. "Great." Slipping out of bed, she bounded into the bathroom.

Rolling onto his stomach, he pressed his face to the pillow, inhaling her scent, then continued off the bed. His feet landed on the hardwood floor with a loud thud.

His inner bear let out a guttural sound. Seeing as Dutchy wasn't in the room, he allowed it. But he warned his animal to behave.

Padding over to the kitchen, he took the platters of food from the refrigerator and shoved them into the oven. The wood fire oven served as the only source of heat in the cabin, and the embers were nearly dying. As he strode over to the pile of wood in the corner, his gaze locked on the CB radio on the desk beside the firewood.

Should check into HQ. No doubt the storm had caught them by surprise too. But then that meant they were probably slammed down there. There was no need to send someone up here right this moment, not when he and Dutchy were safe inside his cabin.

As he threw the firewood into the oven, he imagined they were all-hands-on-deck down in HQ. The chief was probably directing the rangers, making sure there were no lost hikers or shifters. Garret Simpson would—

No.

Not Simpson. He wasn't chief anymore. Not since he retired six months ago.

Damon Cooper was boss now. Commander Cooper. Just like old times.

When was the last time his commander had visited? Even if he did remember, he wouldn't be able to pinpoint the date. Time and days didn't have any meaning to him. He only knew the passage of time based on the seasons changing.

When the commander found him all those years ago, he'd brought him here, to his hometown. Convinced him to join the rangers with him. Said it would be good for him, to be up here in nature and to be around others like them. He'd grown up in a small town in Minnesota, outside Duluth with his family before joining the Special Forces. But he couldn't go back to them, not in his state, so he took up Cooper's offer. The training was a breeze, compared to what he had gone through, and in the end, Garret Simpson gave him the permanent position of guarding the entrance to Contessa Peak. The old man had been perceptive, knew that he would thrive here, away from people.

Of course, he was probably privy to his service records and knew what really happened back in Kargan.

It was his job, what he'd signed up for when he joined the Special Forces. Intelligence had sent them info about a terrorist cell hiding in the basement of the market building, so Cooper sent Krieger and his team of five inside to investigate. But it turned out to be a trap, and the place was rigged with explosives. It crashed around him and his team. Being the only shifter, he managed to survive, but his human team wasn't so lucky. It took three days to dig him out, but by then, it was too late for his men. They died around him. Slowly. Painfully.

But the old chief didn't know what happened after. No, no one knew. Only Damon.

"John?"

Her sweet voice shook him out of the past. Turning, he saw her standing in the bathroom doorway, clad in his shirt again, her hair damp from her shower. "Good?"

The smile that lit up her face was worth everything he had gone through to be here now. "It was heavenly. Thank you. I didn't use up all the hot water, in case you wanted a shower too."

He grunted his thanks. "Food's just heating up."

"Do you have any more coffee?"

"Sure."

As he prepared the brew, she sat down at the table. "Any word about the roads? Is the radio working?"

Guilt poured through him, but he squashed it down. "Not yet. With the sudden storm, I imagine they're busy down there."

"Um ... do you have anyone who might be looking for you? Wondering if you're lost. Or why you haven't gone back home?"

His back stiffened. "No." He turned around. "Why would they?"

She looked relieved. "Good." Her hand slapped over her

mouth. "I mean. Sorry. For the way that sounded. I just ... I should have asked. If you had a ... uh, girlfriend or something."

It took him a second to figure out what she was asking. "No. No one." His mouth went dry as his bear reared up, but he needed to know. "And you?"

"No." She shook her head. "No one like that."

He'd never felt relief like he did now. Not even when they pulled him from the rubble of what was left of that market.

She flashed him a shy smile. "So ... um, do you like being a ranger?"

Did he like it? He wasn't sure what to say. "It's my job." That came out gruffer than he'd liked. "It's good."

"Ah." Her teeth bit into her lush lower lip.

"Just got the fire going again." He nodded at the oven. "Food's warming up."

"Do we only have eggs and bacon?"

"There's other stuff in the pantry. And some steaks and potatoes in the fridge." HQ always sent plenty of food every week. He didn't need anything fancy, but as a shifter, he needed plenty of fuel.

"Oh. That's nice that they keep this cabin stocked for emergencies."

Emergencies?

"I mean, I'm not complaining. Steaks and potatoes sound good. But some veggies would be nice too. Preferably cooked by a professional and served to me by a waiter. I'd even settle for Chinese takeout or a pizza." She chuckled. "I can't cook to save my life, I'm afraid. Ironic, since my aunt owns one of the best pie shops in town."

"Pie shop?"

"You haven't been?"

"No." He'd never been into Blackstone town. Sure, he'd heard the other guys talk about Main Street, but never had the inkling to go. During his year of training, he kept to himself in the barracks the rangers provided.

"We should go." Her eyes lit up. "Aunt Rosie is the sweetest person in the world, you'll love her. And her pies. All made fresh daily by hand. My favorite is cherry with extra whipped cream. Plus, my other aunt's dress shop is just down the street. You can meet them both at the same time."

He stared at her, the wheels in his head turning. When she didn't say anything, he realized she was waiting for an answer for him.

"I mean. If you want." Her shoulders sank, and she curled her body inward, her gaze dropping to her lap.

She wanted him to leave the mountains. Come down to town. Meet her family. It dawned on him that she assumed this was some kind of emergency shelter for rangers. Not his actual home.

The look of hurt on her face from his silence was evident, and his bear threatened to tear him up, angry that he had been the one to put it there. Pushing his bear deep inside, he cleared his throat. "Pie sounds good." It wasn't a lie. But it wasn't quite the truth she wanted, either.

A small smile curled up at the corners of her mouth, and the tension between them eased. "I promise, Aunt Rosie and Aunt Angela are super nice. They're the reason I moved here. To Blackstone. I got my fashion design degree from Parsons in New York, and I was doing all these dead-end internships. I came to visit one time and ... I don't know. Something about this place just called to me, you know? My aunts seemed happy here, even though they moved away from our skulk from Connecticut." She curled a lock of red hair around a finger. "I thought, I would be too. The cost of living was low enough, and I had already started my business online, creating a few pre-made pieces and taking commissions. Then I met these girls, and I eventually designed their wedding dresses. I wasn't really keen on making wedding dresses and I didn't want to compete with Aunt Angela, but she assured me we have different markets. Then when I made Sybil Lennox's dress last year, things just kind of exploded and...."

He listened to her talk, fascinated by how animated and passionate she was about her work. Every word absorbed in his brain—how could it not? While he was proud of her and what she had accomplished, his stomach knotted at the realization that she already had her own life. Outside this cabin. Filled with dinners out and parties. With friends and family.

Idiot.

Of course she had her own life. What did he expect? That she would live here with him, in the middle of nowhere, away from everything and everyone she knew just because he was too fucked up in the head to be around other people?

That selfish part of him said, yes. He could make her happy. Devote his days and nights to giving her pleasure and serving her every need. Up here. Away from everyone.

But he knew that wouldn't last. It couldn't. Couldn't trap her here. She didn't deserve that. This was his prison. Not hers.

"John?" Her head cocked to the side.

"Food should be hot." Turning his back to her, he went to the oven and took out the platters of food.

"You'll burn yourself!" she cried as she came up behind him.

The heat from the platters seared his fingertips. "It's fine." He dropped them on the counter. "It'll heal."

"Silly man." With a sigh, she wrapped her hands around his wrists and kissed his fingers. Lifting her head, she stared up at him, those beautiful light blue eyes boring right into his soul.

How could he give her up? But how could he trap her here? His bear fought him, raging inside him. She must have sensed it as her auburn brows drew together, but he quickly shut his animal away.

"John—"

He silenced her with a kiss. A deep, rough kiss that demanded her attention. Arms wrapped around his neck, and he lifted her up so he could carry her back to bed. This would have to be enough for now. He would enjoy her body and her company. Maybe the snowstorm would continue on. Forever. And he wouldn't have to face the sobering reality that lay ahead for them.

———

Another night had passed, and when Krieger woke up the next day, his stomach filled with ice. He didn't have to look out the window to know that the storm had passed. He just did.

His arms tightened around Dutchy. Just a little longer. He would hold on to her as long as he possibly could. But eventually he would have to let go.

He breathed in her scent, committing this moment to memory. The softness of her skin, the way her curves fit into his body, how her coppery hair caught aflame in the morning light. Lashes fluttered as she opened her eyes. "John?"

Rolling her under him, he caught her mouth in a kiss. He savored it, the taste of her. The feel of her. She moaned, and her thighs parted, allowing him access. He slipped into her, knowing this could be the last time.

She was magnificent. The sex was phenomenal. Their movements were quick and frantic, but he was determined to make it last, letting her come at least twice before he let go for the last time, marking her deep inside, even as she left an indelible mark on him.

Bliss glazed over her eyes and her face lit up with her smile.

"Hmmm ..." Her hands ran down his chest, raking over his skin. "What a way to wake up."

Don't let go.

Don't leave me.

He rolled over, away from her. "I need to go ... to the bathroom."

"Hmm-kay, but can I take a shower after? Or you want to join me?"

"Maybe," he mumbled as he padded toward the bathroom. After cleaning up and finishing his business, he strode out. The bed was empty as Dutchy strode toward the front door.

"John, look!" She threw the door open, stepped out, spread her arms, not caring that she was completely naked. "Oh. It's beautiful out here."

"Yes." He swallowed the lump growing in his throat as he soaked in the sight of her.

"Storm's passed." She gave a little shiver and then hopped back across the threshold, closing the door behind her. "Do you think they can send someone out for us?"

"I'll ask." He lumbered over to the radio and planted himself on the rickety chair. Flipping the switch on, he pressed on the call button. "Base, this is Countess. Can you read me, over?"

A crackle of static broke through the silence. "This is Base. Nice to hear from you, Countess. Hope the storm wasn't too bad for you. Over."

"All good here, Base. But gonna need transport for a stranded guest. Over."

There was a pause before the speakers burst out again. "Roads are still impassable to the peak." Hope surged in him. "But, if your guest can make it to the next station in sector L, we can send someone to meet him up there. Over."

He turned to Dutchy. "Sector L's about a click—a kilometer

—away." He glanced down at her feet. "I don't have shoes for you, you'll have to shift or let me carry you."

"My fox can make that," she said, her tone excited.

"Send transport when you can," he said into the radio. "Over and out." Putting down the receiver, he turned to her. She seemed so happy about leaving here, he almost didn't mind the hole slowly forming in his chest. "When do you want to leave?"

"Can we go now? Oh!" She glanced around. "I don't have any clothes. Do you think there's anything here I can borrow?" She dashed toward the lone closet in the corner.

"You can wear my shirt."

"It's your uniform, I can't take that." She poked her head into the closet. "Besides what are you going to wear? It's—oh!" Her hand pulled out one of his flannel shirts triumphantly. "This should work!" With her excitement, she didn't seem to notice that everything in the closet had been his personal clothes.

Putting on the shirt, she glanced down. "This should do until I get home or I can borrow more clothes." With a grin, she struck a model-like pose with her hands on her hips. "What do you think?"

"Looks ... good."

Her mouth twisted. "I promise, I have better clothes back home. And maybe other things." Her eyebrows wiggled at him. "So, when can we go? Do you need some time to get ready?"

"No." The single word came out in a hoarse whisper. "You can go anytime."

"Great!"

He grabbed his jeans, hopped into them, and followed her outside. She had slipped off the shirt and stood on the porch, naked. "Do you need some space to shift?"

He shook his head and took the shirt from her hands. "I can

make it like this. I'll lead." It would be too dangerous to let his bear out, especially if it caught wind of what he was about to do. "Need to keep your shirt dry."

"Oh. Okay." Turning toward the forest, she stretched her arms out and began her shift. Red and white fur appeared on her skin as she began to shrink. In seconds, a full-grown fox stood where she had been. The little creature did a few turns before settling on its hind legs, looking up at him with curious blue eyes. Dutchy's eyes.

"Pretty little thing." To his surprise, the fox bounded over to him, circling his legs, its bushy red tail brushing his calves. It let out a high-pitched bark when he bent down to stroke its fur. "Hello."

The fox yipped and nuzzled his palm with its dainty snout as its black-tipped ears twitched.

"We should go." He stood up and grabbed the boots sitting by the door. "Follow me, little fox."

They trudged through the snow, with Krieger clearing the way down the rugged path until they reached the main road. The snow was still piled high, and his bear would have made quick work of the blockage, but he needed this. Needed to feel the sweat on his body, the ache in his limbs. The fox followed along, darting about once in a while to sniff at a plant or dig at the dirt, but mostly it stayed by his side, circling his legs or brushing its tail at him saucily.

Finally, they reached Sector L, and the cabin was within his sight. The smoke from the chimney and the light on the porch told him someone was there.

When he halted, the fox ran around his legs in circles before settling in front of him. Slowly, it began to grow, until Dutchy stood in full human form.

"Thanks," she said as he slipped the shirt over her head.

When her face popped through the top, she sent him a dazzling smile. "My fox likes you. A lot."

"I like your fox too." Dread filled his stomach. "Station's right over there."

"All right." She looped her arm through his. "Let's go." When he didn't move, she tugged harder. "John?"

He swallowed. "Won't be going with you."

She frowned. "Don't tell me your boss is sending you out to work. The storm's passed. You've been stuck up there for days. I mean, you haven't been strictly working." She suppressed a smile. "But surely you deserve a couple hours off?"

He didn't know what to say to her. What was he supposed to say? His instincts—his bear—wanted to get down on his knees and beg her to stay. But he couldn't do that to her. Sentence her to a life up here because he and his animal were just too damn broken to function in normal society. "I'm sorry, Dutchy."

"Sorry?"

"I can't. Go with you." Gently, he pried her arm off him. "You should go ... back."

"John?" Her voice shook. "I don't understand what you're saying."

Bile rose in his throat, burning a path from his stomach to his mouth. "You don't ... you don't know me."

"Don't know you? John, what are you saying?" She attempted to reach for him, but he evaded her grasp. "John? Tell me what's the matter."

He stared at her, memorizing the lines and shape of her face. "Nothing. We can't ... Dutchy, you need to go back. And I need to stay here. This is where I belong."

Panic laced her voice. "John, please, tell me what's wrong. We can work it out. We're mates. We need—"

His bear reared up, and he couldn't stop the savage growl from escaping his lips. "No!"

Fear struck Dutchy's face, and she stepped back. "J-John—"

"I didn't—I was—" Maybe this was what had to happen. "Go, Dutchy. I … I can't have you here."

"No, John—"

"I said, go!"

Her face crumpled as she shrank back, and his chest ached so fiercely he couldn't breathe. Control slipped, and he could feel his grizzly slamming its head into his rib cage. He let out a cry as he fought it, but it was too late. *Can't. Let. Her. See.*

With a deep roar, he turned and ran into the trees, as fast as his legs could carry him, fighting the beast inside him. He couldn't let it hurt her. Or anyone. Not again.

In those three days he lay under the rubble, his team slowly dying around him, he vowed to each of them that he would get them the justice they deserved. After they found him and he made a full recovery from his ordeal, he ran off.

It took him the better part of the year to track everyone involved in the market building explosion. Taking down each and every man responsible for the death of five good men plus over a hundred innocent civilians should have satisfied him and his animal. With each kill, he relished in their death. Lived for the thrill of the hunt. But it had only unleashed a darkness in him. It was that wild force that he couldn't control. Made him do something so terrible that it scarred his soul and stained his hands with innocent blood.

And that was the reason he had to be up here, alone. Controlling his killer instinct. *Can't let it happen again.* And certainly not to his mate.

This was his punishment, his cross to bear. And he was never going to let it touch her.

Chapter 4

Heaviness pressed down on Dutchy as she slowly gained consciousness from her dreamless sleep. An invisible weight pushed down on top of her. All over her, plastering her to the bed, making it hard to even open her eyelids.

She lay there, for how long she wasn't sure. Not that it mattered. It was probably past noon. If her bladder hadn't protested so strongly, she wouldn't have moved at all.

Hauling her body out of bed, she trudged to the bathroom, not bothering to flip on any switches in her bedroom darkened by the blackout curtains that remained drawn. The light from the window in the bathroom made her recoil for a second before her eyes adjusted.

After finishing up in the bathroom, she grabbed the sweatpants hanging from the hook on the back of the door. A perfunctory sniff told her it was good enough and she put it on, as well as the matching sweatshirt.

Dragging herself out of the bedroom, she headed to the kitchen. *Water*. There was a half-empty glass still sitting on the counter, so she filled it up from the tap, then downed it before adding it to the growing pile of dishes in the sink.

She ran her fingers through her hair, trying to get the tangles out with not much luck. Shrugging, she padded out into the living room, then stopped. Her nose wrinkled in distaste. Something didn't quite smell right.

Her fox wrinkled its nose and scratched at her, pointing her to the piles of takeout boxes on the coffee table. *Oh crap*. That was from two—no three nights ago. With a sigh, she marched back to the kitchen and grabbed a garbage bag, then headed into the living room to toss the boxes of moldy Chinese food into the bag.

And seeing as she was already on a cleaning kick, she tossed out the other junk on her coffee table, fluffed up the cushions, straightened out the pillows, and put some books back on the shelves.

Hmmm. When was the last time she cleaned up? Too long, based on the layer of dust on the furniture surfaces. A plant in the corner had died a while ago, so she chucked that into the garbage bag too. Then she grabbed the vacuum cleaner from the closet.

By the time she finished cleaning and drew back the curtains to let some sun in, the heaviness pressing on her had lightened.

Huh.

Maybe today was going to be different. Maybe today was the day she could pick herself up. Maybe today was the day she could feel normal again.

She plunked down on the couch, but quickly got up when she felt something poke her butt. Whirling around, she reached in between the cushions and pulled out the offending item but quickly dropped it as if she had picked up a hot iron.

The heaviness pressed down on her again, and her fox hung its head, giving out a pathetic moan.

She didn't even realize her lower lip began to tremble. Or that her hand was shaking.

Stop it!

It's nothing.

It can't hurt you.

It was only a sketchbook after all.

Gingerly, she bent down to pick it up. The problem wasn't the sketchbook itself. No, what made her recoil was what was inside.

The heaviness pressed down on her, threatening to hold her down until she couldn't move. Her lungs squeezed the air from her body, but she clung to the sketchbook tighter.

You can do this. Fight it.

Her body relaxed. Nothing happened. It was just a sketchbook. Hope flittered inside her. Her fox, on the other hand, remained silent.

Look, she told herself. *See what you've done. How far you've come.* Her living room was far from perfect, but it was better. An improvement.

Maybe today was the day.

No, not maybe.

It would be *today*.

Before she lost all nerve, she tucked the sketchpad under her arm, as well as a box of colored pencils on the console table, and strode out of the living room, making a beeline for the front hall. She grabbed her keys and opened the front door.

It was a beautiful, crisp autumn day. When was the last time she had been out? She took a deep breath. Too long. It was too painful to look outside, especially during this time of the year when she knew the leaves were turning. She kept her head down as she headed for her car. *The park.* Yes, she'd head there, to one of her favorite spots in all of Blackstone.

Soon she was pulling into an empty parking spot in Lucas

Lennox Park. She crossed the lawn, heading to the row of benches on the other side, which offered a breathtaking view of the mountains. Her fox bared its teeth and barked viciously.

Ignoring her animal, she reached for the sketchpad and opened it to the front page. Her heart pounded, and her throat felt dry and panic rose in her. *No, please.* How long was this going to go on?

Someone plopping down on the bench next to her made her startle. The young woman was staring up at the mountains, so mesmerized she didn't realize Dutchy was there. "Are you all right?" she asked, putting the pad and pencils on her lap.

The woman jerked, her head toward her. *Pretty,* Dutchy thought. A few years younger than her, maybe. Her pale hair flowed around her, but what caught Dutchy's gaze were the tears pooling in her eyes.

"Um, yeah, I guess." She quickly wiped the tears away. "Sorry, was I disturbing you?"

Dutchy sighed. "No, not at all." How could she be disturbed when she wasn't doing anything? "Are you sure you're okay?"

The woman mumbled something, but she didn't hear it. The mountains seemed to call to her again, despite her fox's aversion to them. "Beautiful, aren't they?"

"Yeah. They are."

They didn't talk anymore as they both beheld the sight before them. Time passed. How long, she didn't know. Shadows passed over the mountains, indicating that the sun was setting. As long as she kept her mind blank, her fox didn't protest or make a sound. As long as she didn't think of—

"Are you an artist?"

Dutchy hummed, not sure how to answer.

"Do you come here often? To draw the mountains?"

She shook her head. "No, I don't draw landscapes."

"What are you doing, then?"

What was she doing? That was a question she asked herself a lot. As her life crumbled around her, every day she wondered what she was doing.

Turning to the mountains, the gaping hole in her heart grew even bigger. She swallowed the lump in her throat. "Trying to find color."

The truth rang in her head as she stared down at the pad in her hand. She didn't fear what was inside the pages. No, she feared what *wasn't* in there.

Nothing.

Pages and pages of nothing.

"Miss? What's wrong?"

Her fox hissed with anger. "I have to go." She bounced to her feet and dashed away as fast as her shifter abilities could take her. She didn't even know where she was going, and she had dropped the pad and pencils somewhere along the way.

A knife-like pain stabbed her in the chest. No, today wasn't the day she was going to turn her life back around. It wasn't the day she would pick up the pieces that had slowly been falling away.

This was her life now. Colorless. Literally. Wherever she looked, she could only see shades of gray, black, and white. What a fucking joke. How could she design and find inspiration when she couldn't see color?

At some point she had shifted into her fox's body, and she felt relief that it could just take over. The fox ran through the trees, jumping over roots, diving through piles of leaves. In animal form, she could forget herself. In the beginning, when she started losing the color, this had been her comfort. It was fading slower as a fox, but eventually its world turned black and white too. But in here, at least, she could still smell and taste and feel.

Run. Run as fast as you can. Not that she could outrun the shadow that loomed over her. It was like a raincloud she couldn't escape. Not since that day her soul tore in half. It sent her into a spiral, into a hole she'd been desperately trying to crawl out of for months.

Maybe today *was* the day.

The day she gave up.

Chapter 5

I f someone told him months ago that he'd be out and about, getting a drink at a bar, Krieger would have laughed in their faces.

But here he was, at the local watering hole, staring into a tall glass of frothy, ice-cold beer. Of course, he was in a private room in the back, far from the noise and din of the main bar, all by himself.

Change didn't happen overnight, after all.

But he was working on it. Bit by bit.

As he took a sip from his beer, the man who strode into the room caught his attention. His bright green gaze immediately landed on Krieger.

"Chief," he greeted as Damon Cooper walked over and sat on the chair across from him.

"Krieg."

They said going through a traumatic event could bring people together. If that were true, then he and Cooper couldn't possibly be closer than if they were actual blood brothers from the same womb. Both of them had gone through a lot—together and apart—and sitting here, in the outside world was a miracle for them both.

There were very few people in the world Krieger would do anything—and he meant anything—for, and his former commander was one of them. Though the chief didn't know it, he'd saved Krieger's life more than once, and he continued to pull him from the darkness by simply being there.

"What's this about?" Krieger asked.

Damon shrugged. "I only know what I told you." He glanced around the empty room. When a particularly loud shout from the riotous group of girls from the outside pierced their little sanctuary, the chief winced. Krieger felt The Demon —Damon's bear—complain furiously, but it didn't explode in rage. It was from The Demon that Krieger's own bear took its cue, remaining still inside him.

Damon raised a dark brow but didn't say anything. Krieger took another sip of his beer.

Yes, change didn't happen overnight, but by working hard, he had come far—much farther than he'd ever have gotten by himself or staying locked up all alone.

Hopefully, he would be good enough. *Soon.* The change would be complete, and he could finally be whole again. Just like Damon. He looked forward to that day. Dreamed about it almost every night. Dreamed about *her.*

Heavy footsteps approaching made them both go on alert, but when they saw who it was, they relaxed. Tim Grimes, owner of The Den and polar bear shifter, lumbered toward them, a mug of beer in one hand.

"Can I top you off, Krieger?" Grimes asked, eyeing his half-empty mug.

"Nah. I'm good."

The polar bear shifter placed the mug in front of Damon

before settling himself on the empty chair on Krieger's right. "All right then. Did you tell him why I called, Chief?"

"Briefly," Damon said. "But why don't you start from the beginning?"

Grimes stroked his bushy white beard with his thumb and forefinger. "My friend Oscar's been missing for three weeks now."

"Did you report it to the Blackstone Police Department?" Krieger asked.

Grimes let out a loud huff. "His nephew did, but they got nothin' so far. Besides, I don't trust cops."

Krieger drummed his fingers on the table. "Then why come to Damon?"

"Oscar's a raccoon shifter," Grimes replied. "Likes to spend time up in the mountains. Sometimes he goes there for days."

"A couple of the rangers have seen him in the past," Damon said. "But nothing recently."

"The peak is his favorite place," Grimes explained. "Says he likes the quiet up there."

Krieger could relate to that. "Hmmm. I do recall a raccoon scent that pops up every now and then. Could be your friend."

"Do you remember when you last scented him?"

A couple of months ago, before he started venturing down the mountains, he probably could have. But now, his memory was filled with scents of the various shifters, hikers, and even his coworkers. "Can't say I do."

"Are you sure he didn't just pack up and leave?" Damon asked. "Or do you suspect something else?"

Grimes's nostrils flared. "Oscar's not like that. Sure, he gets in his cups sometimes, but that's because he lost his mate a couple years ago and hasn't been the same since. Going up to the mountains helps calm him down."

Krieger's hands curled into fists under the table, and it took all his control to pull his bear back from reacting. They knew what that was like, after all.

Grimes continued. "Could he have decided to leave Blackstone on a whim? Possible, but unlikely. According to his nephew, his trailer's untouched. Clothes and keepsakes are there, nothing missing."

Damon's eyes sparked. "Accident then?" His brows furrowed. "I can ask my men to keep an eye out. Though if it's been three weeks, we would have found a trace of him."

Krieger was intrigued now. He patrolled his area religiously and thoroughly. He would have found a lost—or dead—hiker or shifter in that time. "Foul play?"

The implication sent the tension in the room spiking. If someone was harming shifters in the Blackstone Mountains, there would be hell to pay. The burning, dragon type. The Lennoxes would not take such an insult lying down.

"I'll definitely look into this, Tim," Damon promised. "You have my word."

"I appreciate it, Chief." Grimes pushed his chair away and got up. "If you don't mind, I should get back to work. Can I get you anything else?"

"I'm good," Damon said.

Krieger shook his head.

Grimes nodded, then turned and walked away.

"This could be serious stuff," Damon said when they were alone.

"Or nothing at all."

"True. It could be nothing, and I don't want to cause a panic or bother the big boss with this."

The big boss was, of course, Matthew Lennox, the biggest and baddest dragon and Alpha in town.

"What does your gut say, Chief?"

"I'm not sure ... it could be ..." He took a swig of the beer.

The hesitation in Damon's eyes was obvious, and Krieger once again reminded himself that change couldn't happen in an instant. It wasn't a wonder that Damon had risen up quickly in the Special Forces. His instincts and relentlessness had been a force to be reckoned with. But that last mission that had put them both in a similar state had obviously wrecked the former commander's confidence when making calls.

"How about I keep an eye out for anything strange going up there?"

"I think that would be the smart move," Damon said. "I know I can trust you, Krieger."

He grunted. "I'll try not to let you down."

Damon forced a laugh. "Again, it could be nothing, and Oscar'll show up back in town."

"Hope so." He finished his beer.

"Well, I should get going." Damon checked his watch. "Anna Victoria's finishing up her last class, and we're gonna get dinner on Main Street. Want to join us?"

Krieger's body tensed at the mention of the female. "Nah. Wouldn't want to horn in on your date."

"Not at all. In fact, Anna Victoria's been asking when she's going to get to see you again." There was a light in Damon's eyes whenever he said his mate's name. "She thinks you clean up nice in that tux."

He stifled the urge to wince. Attending the Blackstone Ranger anniversary party had been one of the most difficult things he had to do, but he got through it. He didn't stay very long and he had been cocooned in the safety of the company of the four men he trusted most, but he made it. And it brought him so much closer to what he wanted.

"Another time, maybe." He was happy for his former commander that he'd found the other half of his soul and had seen the changes it had made for him. And it was Damon finding his mate that had started this whole thing in the first place.

Damon stood up. "All right, don't be a stranger now."

"I'll head out with you."

The two men walked toward the main room. Thankfully, there weren't too many patrons. However, Krieger immediately noticed Damon tense. "What—oh."

Sitting by himself at the bar, hunched over a glass, was Anders Stevens.

"What the fuck is he doing here?" The Demon growled from deep within. "That asshole's supposed to be at work. I'm gonna tear him—"

"Hold on, Chief." Krieger placed a hand on the other man's shoulder.

"But—"

"You said it yourself, he's one of the best guys you have," Krieger reminded him.

"Yeah, except he's had his head up his ass this entire week. Can't do a damn thing right."

"Why don't you let me take care of this one? Anna Victoria wouldn't want you to be late."

Conflict flashed across Damon's face as the part of him that was chief of the Blackstone Rangers and his mated bear fought with each other. But Krieger already knew which part would win out. "Are you sure about him? What you told me?"

"Sure as day." Ever since he started going to The Den a few months ago, Krieger never missed a chance to observe Blackstone's resident "player" in action. Or lack of action.

While most people thought Anders Stevens was a playboy who took a different girl to bed every night, Krieger knew better. The man was a savior—and all those tipsy girls he took "home" had been safely delivered, unmolested, back to their respective residences. When he reported back to

Damon what he'd found out, he'd been shocked to say the least.

"Tell him to get his ass to work," Damon ordered. "I'll come by your cabin on Friday." Damon made sure to come up and visit at least every other week.

"Sure thing, Chief." He waited until Damon disappeared through the exit before walking over to Anders. It seemed a group of girls playing at the pool table had caught his eye, as he made a move to stand up.

Krieger placed a heavy hand on his shoulder to stop him. "Fancy meeting you here."

Anders's spine stiffened, then he looked up. "Krieger." His mouth pulled back tight. "Yeah, what a coincidence. Are you stalking me?" He tsked. "People are gonna start to talk." He brushed off Krieger's hand. "If you'll excuse me—"

"That"—he nodded toward the girls at the pool table—"is not going to help." Something about Anders set off his instincts. For one thing, that was real alcohol in his glass. And for another, none of those girls looked tipsy, nor were they in danger from anyone in the bar.

"Mind your own business, Sarge," Anders said in a calm tone that held a deadly edge.

"Damon's concerned about you. You know, he thinks you're one of the best rangers we have." Those words had their desired effect—to unnerve and unarm Anders. So, Krieger continued. "But he noticed you've been getting sloppy this last week. I said I'd watch out for you."

"Well, thank you very fucking much, guardian angel. But I don't need your help." Anders reached for the glass of whiskey.

"That's not going to solve anything either. You *know* that." He had no idea why Anders didn't drink, but he knew there had to be a reason. And he would do his best to make sure the tiger shifter didn't fall off the wagon.

"Yeah, well it sure won't fucking hurt."

As he lifted the glass to his lips, Krieger considered swatting it out of his hand, but there was no need. Anders stopped halfway; his attention caught by something by the door.

No, it wasn't something. It was someone.

A woman.

Of course.

Krieger had seen that look in Anders's face before. It was the same one he'd observed several times these past months. Damon. Gabriel Russel. Daniel Rogers. Every single one of them had that expression on their faces whenever their mates were around. Like there was no one else in the room—or the entire world.

When the woman spotted Anders and started making a beeline toward them, Krieger decided it was probably better to give them some privacy. "I'm gonna head to the john."

He strode off toward the men's bathroom, thankful that it was empty. The din outside wreaked havoc on his senses, making his bear antsy. Still, it was a testament to how far he'd come. How the work he'd put in the last few months was paying off.

Change didn't happen overnight. And he'd worked his fucking ass off the last couple of months, crawling out of that hole he'd dug himself into for the past five years. Slowly leaving his self-constructed prison up in the peak. Opening up to Damon. Watching over his colleagues. Keeping them safe. All to make himself a better man. To be worthy of his mate.

And maybe soon, he would be.

The door pushed open, knocking him out of his thoughts. His grizzly didn't even bare its teeth or growl in the direction of the stranger who came in. If it had been a year ago, it would have fought him, clawed at him to lash at anyone who dared come into their space. Hell, a year ago, he wouldn't have made it this far away from his cabin for this long. Now, he could even look himself in the mirror without feeling anger or disgust.

After washing his hands, he strode back outside. Glancing toward the bar, he saw Anders was alone now. Where was the woman? From the way the tiger shifter was giving the exit the thousand-yard stare, he could only guess.

Anders seemingly shook himself out of his daze as he dashed toward the door.

What the hell? "Anders!" he called.

When he caught up to him, Anders stopped and turned around. "I have to go," he said. "Er, sorry, man. Tell Damon he can punish me tomorrow. I'll even do trash duty for a month. But I have to go now."

From the frantic way he left, Krieger could only guess that Anders fucked things up somehow and needed to make it up to his mate. This would be interesting, to see the boisterous and cocky tiger shifter brought down to his knees by his mate.

However, when he got out of The Den, he did not expect to see Anders facing down a luxury limo head-on.

Fucking idiot!

Krieger sprang into action, his animal reflexes kicking in as he tackled Anders to the ground.

"No!" Hands reached out to claw at him. "Let me go!"

"Anders." Holding the other man down, Krieger reached out to his animal side, its rage burning hotly. "Anders!"

That seemed to work as the fury in his eyes dulled down. "What the fuck, man!" He wrenched himself away. "They took her, Goddammit! Took my mate!"

"And how would getting flattened by that car have helped?" Krieger snorted. "Use your fucking head." Still, he couldn't blame Anders.

"I need to go after them." He shot up to his feet and marched toward his pickup.

Krieger let out a grunt. "I'm going with you."

"Whatever," Anders warned. "Just don't get in my way."

They both hopped into the pickup, and Anders sped out of the parking lot, tires screeching as he chased after the limousine. His teeth were gritted together and his knuckles white from gripping the wheel, mind seemingly focused on one single task: get his mate. So, Krieger knew he had to be the calm, reasonable one.

Fishing his phone out of his pocket, he dialed 911 and reported the incident. The dispatcher was cool and professional as she took down the details. "...we're in pursuit now, heading northbound on Highway Seventy-Five ... yes, thank you."

The limo was still a small dot down the highway, and Anders let out a frustrated sound as the engine of his truck protested as he pushed it to its limits. "Goddammit!"

"Just keep 'em in sight," he assured the tiger shifter. "We'll get help." While he kept the dispatcher on the line, he switched to his messaging app and sent a text to Damon, giving him a quick rundown of what was happening.

"What the fuck?"

Krieger slammed his palms on the dash as Anders suddenly engaged the brakes. "What the hell?"

Anders's animal growled, and Krieger followed his gaze. The limo they had been pursuing was now slammed up against a massive pine tree on the side of the highway.

The muscles under Anders's skin crawled, and Krieger knew his shift was inevitable. "I'll take the right, you take the left," he instructed. "And do what you can to keep your mate safe."

Anders answered with a savage, inhuman roar as he leapt out of the truck. Krieger whipped his shirt off and shucked out of his jeans and boots as he dashed toward the limo.

Calling on his grizzly, he let the mighty bear tear out of him, skin making way for fur and hulking shoulders. Coming up on the right side of the vehicle, the bear smashed a giant paw through the window, then pulled the entire door off. Then it poked its head in and let out a defining roar. To his surprise, a large, burly man flew out, tackling him to the ground.

Fucking idiot.

Despite putting up a big fight, the male was no match for the bear. Oh, he was fierce and fought well, and Krieger could sense the other man was a shifter, too, but that didn't mean shit when faced with a thousand-pound beast. However, as he always did before he had to take a life now, he had to tell himself this was necessary, to protect a friend and prevent another death of an innocent. With that in mind, he finished the job.

The roar of a tiger and the pathetic cry that followed it told Krieger that Anders took care of things on his end as well.

As the bear stood over its kill, it suddenly went very still. The beast turned and lumbered back toward the highway. The sirens in the distance were coming closer, but that wasn't what caught his bear's attention.

And when he saw the flash of coppery red on the gray asphalt, his heart stopped beating.

No.

"No!"

Krieger didn't even realize he'd begun to shift as he raced toward the middle of the highway. By the time he reached the prone body lying on the ground, he was fully human, and he cradled Dutchy's frail, naked body in his arms.

"No ..." Tears sprung in his eyes, and he was powerless to stop them. "Please. No." He brushed the hair covering her pale face, not that he needed to confirm it was her. He just knew, just as his bear did. "Don't leave me. I'm sorry. I'm sorry I couldn't be better."

"... what the hell happened?"

"... kidnapped Darcey...."

"... went after them ... and Krieger...."

"... shit. I need to go check on Sarah. Will he be okay?"

"Yeah, I'll stay here."

That last voice Krieger recognized as Damon's. And the other man who strode down the hallway of the Blackstone Hospital was Daniel Rogers.

What happened after he found Dutchy on the road was all a blur to him. The sirens growing louder. The EMTs trying to get to Dutchy. It took a couple of officers to pull him off. The sharp sting of a tranq dart. Not that it knocked him out, but it was enough to keep him down until Damon arrived on the scene. Then, the sight of Dutchy being loaded away onto a stretcher sent him and his animal into a frenzy again.

Damon promised that he would drive him to the hospital if he calmed down. And so, here they were.

"You okay, man?" Damon asked as he sat beside him. They were in some kind of waiting room, but even here, the sterile smell of the hospital burned at his nostrils. "Are you ready to talk?"

He swallowed hard. Though he and Damon had built up their friendship in the last months, this was the one thing he couldn't share with the other man. It seemed too private and personal, plus he didn't want Damon to push the mate thing, not when he wasn't ready.

"Krieger?"

"You saved my life," he began.

Damon chuffed. "I sent you into that market building. Right into a trap. You were buried under there for days. I hardly call that saving your life."

"It was war. You get faulty intelligence now and again. But I'm not talking about that part." He flexed his fingers on his knees. "I'm talking about when you brought me here. After ..." He pushed away the memories. "You gave me a place where I could stay away from other people. Because I couldn't control my animal's thirst for blood." And that was the truth. When Damon found him, he'd been in a feral state, living deep in the mountains of Kargan in mostly animal form. The locals had thought he'd been some kind of monster. And he was.

"But you're better now," Damon pointed out. "You've come so far. I mean, look at where you are now."

"Remember that day you told me that you found your mate?"

The chief's jaw hardened. "I would have lost her, if it wasn't for you." Anna Victoria had been kidnapped by her ex-fiancé who had chased her down because she was a key witness in a crime he committed. Krieger had found her right before the bastard's goons could do the deed and he took care of them. "So, you can consider that debt paid."

"But you saved my life again." He lifted his head to meet his friend's gaze. "I saw for myself the change that happened to you. And that's when I realized I was wrong. Wrong for pushing Dutchy away. To think I couldn't change for her."

Damon swallowed hard. "This ... was all for her?"

He nodded, then hung his head low. "And now it's too late."

"Krieger, no." Damon put a tentative hand on his shoulder. "It's not. She'll be fine." He squeezed gently. "She's a shifter, right? Met her once, you know. She seemed a little sad. What happened there?"

And so, he told Damon everything. About finding her in the snow all those months ago. How his bear instantly knew who she was. And how he pushed her away. "You know why I had to do that. I couldn't force her to choose between a life of isolation with me and her real life out here. It wouldn't have been fair. She would have resented me."

"Jesus." Damon sucked in a breath. "I had no idea. Listen—"

"Are you the family of Duchess Forrester?"

Krieger shot to his feet at the sound of the voice. "How is she, Doc?" He said to the older man clad in a white coat. The ID around his neck identified him as Dr. Charles Jenkins.

"And you are?"

"He's her mate," Damon offered.

The doctor relaxed. "She's stable after the surgery. They just moved her into a private room. Four-oh-five. I need to tell you something, though. She's—"

Krieger didn't bother to wait for the doctor to finish his sentence. He tore down the hallway, giving the room numbers a cursory glance as he tracked down 405. Bursting into the room, he skidded to a halt at the sight before him.

Dutchy lay on the bed, looking frail and thin, dressed in a drab hospital gown. A machine was hooked up to her nose and mouth helping her breathe, and her left arm was bound in a cast.

A cold wave washed over him. Dr. Jenkins said she'd been in surgery. But why? She was a shifter. He guessed the limo had struck her, but she was still alive when he'd found her. She should have healed with minimum help, even with internal injuries.

"Sir!" Dr. Jenkins, a few nurses, and Damon came into the room.

A growl escaped his lips as he slowly pivoted toward the doctor. "What's wrong with her? Why isn't she healing?" He took a menacing step forward. "What did you do?"

Damon immediately put himself between him and the staff. "Krieger, stand down."

"Look at her! She's—"

"Stop!" The Demon was there now, waiting at the edges of Damon's consciousness. "And listen to what he tried to tell you."

Dr. Jenkins cleared his throat. "As I was trying to say, Ms. Forrester's shifter healing isn't kicking in as fast as we'd hoped."

"Why?" Krieger growled.

"There may be several reasons, but I won't know for sure until she wakes up. I was surprised myself when they brought her in. I thought she was a human and performed the necessary surgery on her."

"Will she be okay?" Damon asked.

"She's still under observation," Dr. Jenkins said. "But I think she will recover. Slowly. Like any human patient."

Krieger turned back to his mate. The rise and fall of her chest reassured him somewhat, but that didn't answer any questions.

"Is this the—Oh my God!"

An older redheaded woman had strolled in carefully, but when her gaze landed on Dutchy, she let out a sharp cry and rushed to her side. "Dutchy ... my darling girl." Leaning over, she pressed a kiss to Dutchy's pale forehead and clutched her limp hand. "Thank you for calling me, Damon. Angela's on her way here, too, she's just closing up her shop."

"Of course, Rosie," Damon said somberly.

"You said she'd been in an accident?" She turned to Dr. Jenkins. "How is she? What happened?"

So, this was Rosie. Dutchy's aunt. He could see some resemblance, especially with the hair and the eyes. She was wearing one of those vintage-style dresses and from the name plate still pinned to her chest, it was obvious she had rushed here from work.

"... and now we can only wait," Dr. Jenkins concluded.

"She'll pull through. My girl is strong." Curious pale blue eyes flickered to Krieger. "And you are?"

Krieger swallowed, unable to speak. Those blue eyes ... they looked so much like Dutchy's that his stomach hurt.

"This is Krieger," Damon began as he walked up to Rosie and placed a hand on her shoulder. "He and Anders found Dutchy after she'd been hit by that car. That's another long story Anders can tell you about, but ... turns out Krieger is Dutchy's mate." Damon had obviously been careful in selecting his words so they didn't come out as a lie.

Rosie gasped, and she covered her mouth. "Oh." Circling around the bed, she came up to him and embraced him. "Thank goodness. You came to her at the right time."

He stood in the old woman's embrace awkwardly, unsure of what to do. When she let go, she raised a brow at him. "You've never been to my pie shop, have you?"

"N-no, ma'am."

A weak smile formed on her face. "We'll have to remedy that, won't we? When she wakes up."

Not if. *When*. "Yes."

Dr. Jenkins cleared his throat. "We should leave her to rest."

Neither Krieger nor his bear liked that idea, so he grabbed the nearest chair and dragged it next to Dutchy's bed. "I'll stay here."

Dr. Jenkins frowned. "There's no need for that. We have nurses here who'll watch over her. You can't do anything more for her than they can."

Ignoring the doctor, he sat down, bracing his elbows on his knees.

"Sir, I insist—"

"I said, I'll stay here."

"Dr. Jenkins," Rosie said in a soothing voice. "It's all right. Maybe ... maybe it will be good for her. He's her mate, after all."

Dr. Jenkins harrumphed. "Fine. In any case, I'll need you to fill out some paperwork for her."

"Of course, Doctor."

Krieger stopped paying them any mind, not even when they said goodbye or when Damon came up to him and told him to take all the time he needed. No, his gaze was fixed on his mate, as if doing so would magically heal her and she would open those beautiful eyes.

What happened to you, Dutchy?

Chapter 6

Dutchy drifted in and out of the darkness, like flotsam pulled up and down by stormy ocean waves.

"... why isn't she healing faster ..."

Beep ... beep ... beep

"... my poor girl ..."

Drip ... drip ... drip

"... haven't left her side ... go take a break ..."

Each time she reached for the surface, the current only pulled her back. Part of her wanted to be lost, to be dragged down to the bottom of the sea where she wouldn't have to feel anything anymore.

But another part of her urged her to fight.

And when her eyes opened, it was as if her soul had been hauled back into her body.

The first thing she felt was the burning pain down her throat. Her first instinct was to pull at the intrusion pushing in her mouth, but when she tried to raise her hands, found them restrained. Panic welled in her as she attempted to cry out.

"She's awake!" A familiar feminine voice shouted. "Call the nurse!"

Hands held her down. Something plastic and snake-like was removed from her windpipe. Her body relaxed as air filled her lungs again.

Slowly, her lids opened. Two familiar faces leaned over her, both weary, but smiling.

"You're awake," Aunt Angela said, her voice trembling.

A warm hand smoothed over her forehead, the scent of pastry and sugar drifting down to her nostrils. "I knew you'd pull through, dear girl," Aunt Rosie added.

Dutchy opened her mouth to speak, but her mouth and throat were dry and scratchy. "Wa ... ter ..."

Angela sprang into action and grabbed a cup from the table, pressing it to her lips as Rosie propped up her head. "Slowly, Dutchy," she cooed. "I know, I know ... but you don't want to choke."

The cool water soothed her dry mouth and throat, and though she protested when Angela took the cup away, she nonetheless felt grateful for the small bit of relief. Easing back down on the bed, she stared at the ceiling. *Where am I? What happened?* She shut her eyes tight. The restraints on her wrists were gone, but something tight wrapped around her left arm that made it hard to move.

"You're in the hospital," Rosie said, as if hearing her thoughts. "There was an accident."

Accident? The days and weeks during the past couple of months melded together, she couldn't pinpoint how she could have—

The memories flooded back. Of that day in the park. Of hope flourishing in her as she attempted to spark her creative soul. And the crushing disappointment at another blank page. Tears gathered at the corner of her eyes, spilling over as a sob tore at her throat.

"It's all right, dear girl." Callused fingers brushed the tears from her cheeks. "Everything's going to be fine. We're here."

She didn't want to be here. She just wanted it all to go away. To be left alone. Her fox trilled sadly, its body limp and tired.

"Dutchy?" Angela's voice pierced through her skull. "Darling? Are you having trouble opening your eyes?"

"Maybe she's just tired," Rosie offered. "She needs rest."

"But I don't understand. She's been here for three days. How could she not be completely healed by now?"

Three days?

"Maybe it's—oh, you're back. She just woke up."

A soft growl made her skin tingle. "Woke up? Why didn't anyone—" Heavy footsteps stomped closer. "Dutchy?"

Her eyes flew open at the third presence in the room. It took a few second for her synapses to make the connection.

No!

Her fox reared up defensively.

John Krieger blew out a breath as he came up beside the bed. "You're awake."

He reached out, and the moment his hand touched her shoulder, her animal hissed as its claws raked at her insides, pushing to get out.

"No!" She jerked up and would have jumped off the bed if Rosie hadn't caught her in her arms and held her down. "No!" The vixen barked and yowled at him, baring sharp teeth. It wanted out. It wanted *blood*. And because her body was too weak for the shift, it tried to forcefully claw its way out.

Krieger stared at her, his dark brows knitting together. "Dutchy, it's me—"

"Get ... away." Panic rose in her as Krieger reached for her again, and her fox snapped its teeth at him. She clung to her aunt tighter and her gaze strayed toward the door. "Out!"

"Dutchy, what's going on?" Rosie asked as she buried her face in her shoulder. "He's your—"

"Please," she sobbed. "Make him leave."

"Dutchy, please," Krieger began. "I—"

"You should go," Rosie said. "Angela ..."

"Just until she calms down," Angela said in a soothing voice. "Please, Krieger. Just for a little while until the doctor can see to her."

Seconds ticked by as silence filled the room. But once she heard the heavy footsteps get farther away and the door close, her body relaxed. As Rosie helped her back down on the bed, she could see the confusion on her aunt's face, but she wasn't ready to face her questions yet, so she closed her eyes, pretending to fall asleep until eventually she did drift off.

When she awoke again, the fluorescent light above her burned brighter. Turning her gaze toward the window, she saw only darkness.

"You've been asleep for hours."

Her body tensed, but when she recognized the feminine voice, her muscles relaxed. Rosie stood up from the chair next to her bed and brought a cup with a straw up to her lips. The ice-cold water was a balm to her parched mouth and throat, and this time, Rosie allowed her to drink as much as she wanted.

"Better?" A hand smoothed over her temple.

"Yes," she managed to rasp.

"The doctor would like to come and see you," she said. "If you can manage to stay awake. Otherwise, you can go back to sleep."

She shook her head. The motion made her wince. Pain began to seep into her body, concentrated on her left shoulder, arm, down the right side of her torso, and her ribs. Had she felt this hurt before?

"Are you in pain? The nurses warned me the meds might be wearing off."

Meds? Did shifters even need medicine for pain?

Rosie reached to her other side and pressed on a button by her hand. "There. They'll be here soon."

Only a minute passed before a nurse in scrubs walked in. She babbled as she talked, not really waiting for Dutchy to reply as she plunged a syringe into the IV line.

"... there you go," she said as Dutchy's body relaxed. "Oh, the doctor's here."

Dutchy glanced up at the new person in the room—a tall, older man who wore a white coat. "Ms. Forrester? I'm Dr. Jenkins."

"H-hello, Doctor," she rasped.

"It's all right, no need to overexert yourself. If you don't mind, I'll need to perform a quick examination." He picked up the clipboard at the foot of her bed and placed his stethoscope in his ears.

She nodded and he began to check her pulse, breathing, and her throat and eyes. A nurse came in to check her blood pressure, and when everything was done, he scribbled on the clipboard. "Vitals are good ... tell me, do you remember what happened to you?"

"A little." After the park, she'd shifted and ran off. She couldn't remember where her fox brought her or how long they'd been roaming, but they darted across the highway when something large and blue came from nowhere. "I was hit by a car."

Dr. Jenkins put away his stethoscope. "Yes. It was a good thing that the emergency services were already on the way and they got you here in time for surgery for your internal injuries."

"S-surgery?" Her gut twisted.

"You also have bruised ribs, a dislocated shoulder, a

fractured forearm, not to mention cuts and contusions all over, but thankfully, no head injuries."

"But, I'm a shifter, didn't they tell you? I should be able to heal on my own." Sure, surgery could help in some cases when shifters got really hurt, but usually it wasn't necessary. "How long ago was the accident?"

"Three days ago."

"Three days?" She glanced over at Rosie, who nodded. "How? Why am I not healing?"

"The science of shifter medicine isn't exact because there's just too many factors and too many types of shifters." Dr. Jenkins's expression turned grave. "There have been some cases where if a shifter has a traumatic experience, it can change them fundamentally. Some experience a fracture of sorts, a disconnection from their animals. Their animals may act out, making them difficult to control, akin to going feral. While others experience loss of their healing capabilities or even other senses. Tell me, did anything happen to you recently? And are you feeling any other physical abnormalities, symptoms, or illnesses?"

Shame burned through her. She didn't want to admit what had been happening to her vision, at least not in front of Rosie. "I ... can we do this another time, Doctor? I'm getting tired."

"Of course. I have some more rounds to make before I have to go home, but if you need me at all, just tell the nurses, and they'll call me."

"Thank you, Doctor."

As soon as Dr. Jenkins left, Rosie turned to her, hands on her hips. "Don't you even think about pretending to sleep."

Dutchy already had the blanket halfway up her chest. "I wasn't. I really am tired."

"Duchess Marie Forrester, what aren't you telling him?" Rosie's gaze narrowed on her. "What aren't you telling *me*?"

"Nothing," she said defensively. "Please, Aunt Rosie—"

She moved closer to the bed. "What are you hiding, darling?"

"I said it's nothing. And I'm just fine."

"No, you're not." Rosie rubbed her temple. "You haven't been fine, not for a very long time."

"I'm—"

"Shush!" Her aunt put a hand up. "Don't deny it. Angela and I haven't seen or heard from you in months, but we always thought it was because you were busy with clients. But then Temperance tells me you're not even returning her calls—which is not just bad for business, but rude, because your friends and I sang your praises. And now this ..." She glanced at the door. "He's still out there. Waiting to see you. He says he's your mate. Is that true?"

Blood drained from her face, and her fox howled in displeasure.

Rosie must have sensed it, because she practically jumped away. "Dutchy?" Rosie's brows drew together. "What's the matter? Please tell me. So I can help you."

"Oh, Aunt Rosie." She burst into tears when her aunt gathered her in her arms. "I ... I can't ... I can't be around him."

"Why not? Is he lying? Is he not your mate?"

Her vixen hissed and barked, its claws ripping her up at the mere thought of him or mention of his name. It had been doing that ever since he walked away from her, as if her fox trained her not to think of him. And when he had showed up by her bedside and touched her, it had gone crazy, wanting to attack him. "You felt it, right? Felt how my fox reacted to him when he was in here?"

"But why?" Rosie asked. "You've never even met—oh." She frowned. "He didn't mention you two knew each other before."

She sniffed and wiped her nose with her gown. "Y-you've talked to him?"

"A little bit. He doesn't really say much. But, as I told you, he hasn't left your side, except to eat or clean up, and even then, he probably wouldn't have gone unless Damon was here to nag him." Rosie placed a hand over hers. "What happened between you two?"

A lump formed in her throat, and though she wanted to say something to Rosie, the words wouldn't come out.

"It's all right," Rosie said sympathetically. "You can tell me when you're ready, okay?" She pulled her in for a tight hug. "I'll take care of you. So will Angela."

"Th-thank you. Can you ... don't tell anyone else back home, okay? Especially Mom?" When her human father had passed away when she was little, Belinda Forrester had moved her and her siblings back to her home town to be close to her family and skulk.

It was the ideal situation as the skulk was close-knit, with families living together not unlike a commune, raising their kits alongside each other. Dutchy had loved it and flourished in it as creativity was encouraged, but she moved away for her studies and career. Everyone had celebrated her successes with her, from getting into the most competitive fashion design program in the country to when the gown she designed for Sybil had made it into Vogue. If any one of them found out what had been happening to her in the last couple of months ...

"If that's what you want." Rosie's mouth twisted. "But you'll let me know what I can do to help you, right?"

"Of course."

"I need to go outside for a bit, will you be okay?" Rosie asked. "Do you want anything? Some food, if the nurse says it's okay?"

"Go ahead," she said. "And no ... I'm fine."

"All right." Rosie pressed a kiss to her temple. "I'll see you in a bit."

As soon as she was alone, Dutchy let out the breath she'd been holding. She took several deep, calming breaths. Her vixen yapped and slunked about, as if an enemy would pounce at them at any moment.

I know you're trying to protect me, she told her animal. *But why aren't we healing?* Ever since she started shifting when she was about four or five, she'd never been sick or hurt. And now, she'd been out for three days, and the weakness in her body was nothing like she'd ever felt before.

Was the doctor right? Had she somehow disconnected from her animal? She didn't feel different, other than the fact that her vixen reacted violently to the mere thought of *him,* and it had gone feral when he tried to touch her. Was this the reason why she couldn't access her shifter healing?

Rosie said to tell her what she could do to help, but the truth was, she didn't know how or if anyone could help her, not when she'd given up herself.

Chapter 7

"Can I get you anything? Coffee? A sandwich?" Damon asked. "Did you get anything to eat at all?"

When was the last time he'd eaten? Krieger wasn't sure. What time was it when Dutchy woke up and threw him out of her room? "I'm fine," he mumbled.

"You don't look fine," Damon insisted. "What the hell happened? What are you doing out here?"

What was he supposed to say? That Dutchy woke up and freaked out the moment she saw him? His chest tightened, remembering the sheer pain on her face. But worst of all, he could *feel* her mistrust and loathing at the mere sight of him. His bear, too, raged at the visceral reaction from her, and it did not like it one bit.

"Krieg?"

He looked up at Damon. "Can we talk about something else?" He needed a distraction. Maybe he should have taken Damon up on his offer of food. But his stomach was tied up in knots, and he probably wouldn't have been able to keep anything down, not when things weren't right between him and Dutchy.

Damon sighed and grabbed an empty chair from across the room. "What do you want to talk about?"

"How are things back at HQ?"

His lips pulled back. "I'm short two rangers. How do *you* think things are going?"

He winced. "Sorry. I'll get back as soon as I can—"

"I know." Damon scrubbed a hand down his face. "Look, I meant what I said about you taking the time you need. Hell, you've probably earned it since you've never taken a vacation."

"You said you're short by two people. Who else is down?"

"Who do you think?" Damon sighed. "Stevens. He's working things out with his mate. Shows up sporadically, but basically, he's been hanging around Darcey for days."

The blonde they'd chased down. He'd forgotten about that. "And how are things going?"

"Dunno. Daniel's got the info, but he's tight-lipped. He's hoping they work it out since Darcey happens to be his sister-in-law. By the way, I hope you don't mind, I told him what you told me about Anders and all those girls. At first, he couldn't believe it, but I told him the info came from you, so now he's trying to help reform Anders's playboy image." He let out a chuckle. "Of course, it's not helping his reputation at work. I think some of the guys feel betrayed because they think he's some kind of lady-killer hero."

He huffed. Of course, he understood on some level what that was like. He winced in shame now, but he'd once reveled in the action and thrill of chasing pussy. Women hadn't been in short supply, especially around the base. But that had been a different life. "Did you—"

The door to Dutchy's room opened and immediately, his body went on full alert. But the flash of red hair wasn't his mate's.

"Ma'am," he said to Dutchy's aunt. "How—how is she?"

Rosie eyed him warily. "Awake." She paused, then straightened her shoulders, her pale blue eyes flashing. "What happened between you and my niece?"

Krieger wasn't surprised she'd figured it out. "She didn't tell you?"

"No." Her hands fisted at her sides. "But someone better damn well tell me before I lose my mind, and that someone better be you, young man."

Young man? Sheesh, he hadn't been called young in ages. But the stern look on the female's face—not to mention the fierce determination he could sense in her animal—made it difficult to deny her. "We've ... met before. A few months ago. In that big snowstorm."

And so, he told her what happened. Each word was like reliving the whole damn thing again, but she wanted the truth and so she would have it.

By the time he was done, Rosie's face had gone as red as her hair. "You just ... rejected her? Told her to leave? After what you'd been through together?" Though he didn't give her every detail, she obviously guessed their time together in his cabin wasn't some innocent sleepover. "Tossed her aside like trash when you were done with her?" The words cut deep, but how could he deny it?

"Rosie," Damon warned.

"No." He waved his friend aside. "She's right."

"But she doesn't know. Neither did Dutchy. What happened to you ... it changes a man." Of course, only Damon could understand why he needed to push Dutchy away. He'd gone through it himself. *PTSD was a fucking bitch.*

But he didn't know this was how things would end up. "I'm sorry for hurting her, but I've been working on myself." Didn't she know, change didn't happen overnight? "I was ... I was trying to be better, for her."

Rosie was practically vibrating with anger. "Better for her? Staying with her, completing the mating bond, that would have been better for her!"

He was at a loss for words, and the only thing he could do was apologize. "I'm sorry," he said. "I'm so sorry."

"Your sorry doesn't make her better," Rosie spat. "It won't make her the same again."

"It's not his fault she was run over by a car," Damon reminded her.

Rosie turned a razor-sharp gaze on Krieger. "But it *is* your fault she's not healing."

"Me?" he asked, puzzled.

"It makes sense now. It's the only explanation." Rosie's nostrils flared. "The doctor ... he said some shifters, when they go through a traumatic experience, they can feel disconnected from their animals. Some lose control while other shifters lose their abilities. That's why she's not healing. Because of what you did to her. You broke her!"

Krieger and Damon's eyes met. Based on the chief's face, he knew what he was thinking. They had gone through similar paths after all, and they knew what it was like to lose control of your animal. A hot ball curled up in his chest, making it hard to speak.

"Rosie, please," Damon began as he gingerly put a hand on her arm. "Is there anything I can do? Just say the word."

The fox shifter sighed. "I don't know, Damon. I—" A ringing sound interrupted her and she fished her phone from her purse. "Hello—Angela! Thank goodness. You should come ... all right. Give me a moment." Glancing at the two men, she covered the mouthpiece of her phone. "I need to speak to Angela privately. I'm going to find a quiet corner. Excuse me."

Krieger stared after Rosie as she walked away. "I need to see her, Damon."

Damon's dark brows slashed downwards. "Rosie won't like it."

"Just five minutes. Please ... if she comes back—"

"All right. I'll take care of it," he promised. "Go. You might not have enough time."

Rolling his shoulders back, he reached for the doorknob and turned it slowly. Dutchy was looking outside the window, so she didn't notice him sneak in. He crept quietly, not making a sound. But she must have sensed him approaching because her head turned. Pale blue eyes widened as a myriad of emotions crossed her face, none of them comforting to see.

"Don't—"

He halted and put his hands up. "I won't come any closer. Not if you don't want me to."

She let out a long breath. "I don't want you to. I don't want you here at all."

Each word was like a cut of a razor on his skin. "Please, Dutchy. Talk to me. Tell me what's wrong."

She flinched, like she had been hurt. "I told you to leave."

"I can't. You know that, Dutchy," he said. *Please*, he prayed silently. *Please be all right.*

"You did fine enough these past months," she spat bitterly.

His heart sank, but he deserved that. "Let me explain." He took a tentative step forward. "I had to—"

"No! Stay away!"

"I can't, Dutchy. Not anymore. I'm here now."

"But you have to," she cried. "Please."

"Just tell me what's the matter? Why aren't you healing properly, Dutchy? And why are you scared of me?"

Her lower lip trembled. "Can't you feel it?" she said through gritted teeth. "My animal?"

Wait. *Why didn't I think of that?* Their animals had known instinctively they were meant to be together. *Mine*, he recalled his bear saying the moment he looked into her pale blue eyes. And hers had called to him too. He remembered the pretty little creature, how it had preened for him and flirted as they walked down the mountain. Surely, Dutchy would listen to her animal. So, he reached out to her vixen. "I—"

The reaction he got wasn't what he expected.

Loathing.

Distaste.

Rage.

"Dutchy?" he rasped.

She sobbed. "Can you feel it now? My fox … it hates you."

His bear roared in furious denial.

Chapter 8

Despite what had happened, Dutchy didn't hate Krieger. Sure, she felt used and discarded after being unceremoniously dumped at that ranger station, but sadly, dating in New York had prepared her for that kind of disappointment. No, she understood that despite sexual chemistry and attraction, sometimes a relationship just didn't work out.

But her fox didn't quite agree.

The first few days when she got back home after being trapped in the mountains with him, she had this pathetic fantasy that he'd changed his mind. That he would come after her, tell her he had been wrong to push her away and make some grand gesture to ask for forgiveness. They were mates after all. They were supposed to be together from now on. That's what happened to all her friends—Kate, Amelia, and Sybil. They were all claimed and bonded by their mates and now happy with their families.

But why did John leave them? Why didn't he want to bond with her and start their own brood? Surely, he was feeling the pain of their separation as keenly as she was?

Every shadow she saw, every male she bumped into, she thought was him. Her fox had been hopeful, too, its head and ears perking up each time she thought John was there. But weeks passed, and it was obvious she wouldn't see him again. And that's when her world spiraled. It wasn't a swift plummet to the bottom, rather a slow decent that slowly chipped away at her. What the doctor said ... yes, she did experience a traumatic experience. Her mate's utter rejection.

"Dutchy?" Horror clearly marred his face. "What the hell happened?"

Her lips peeled back. "What do you think? Don't you see, John?" Because for the first time in months, it was finally crystal clear to her. "When you left me, I went into a depression. I tried to claw myself out of it, but the more I struggled, the harder it pulled me down. I lost interest in the outside world, and maybe that's when it lost interest in me." Now that she'd started, she couldn't stop, as if she'd been damming up all her anger and sadness for the past months, and now it was bursting free. "I stopped working because I couldn't find the creative energy to design. I even let down my friends. Then the colors slowly faded. It was so gradual; I didn't notice it."

"What do you mean, the colors faded?"

Shame burned through her, but she continued on. "I mean they're *gone*. I can't see any color at all." She forced herself to stare at him, searching for those indescribable blue eyes, but all she saw was a light shade of gray.

"And your fox ..."

"I told you." Her fox had made its stance clear. John Krieger was the enemy. He had hurt them so deep and so fundamentally that it couldn't stand him. "It doesn't want you around. When you touched me, it tried to claw out of me to get to you." It wanted blood—his. Even now, the vixen stared at him with a deep hostility that burned like a bright star.

He recoiled in horror. "That can't ... you ..." He let out a low, guttural sound as he raked his fingers through his dark hair. "I didn't mean to ..."

When he took another step toward her, her fox fought with all its might, its sharp claws raking at her insides. She curled up into a tight ball. "Please ... John ... just go."

Though her face was buried in her knees, she could feel his stare linger on her. Her body tensed tighter, and it was only when she heard his heavy footsteps and the sound of the door slamming shut that her muscles relaxed.

Tears escaped the corners of her eyes, and once they started, she couldn't stop them. *Oh God.* She just wanted this feeling to stop. Didn't want to deal with this anymore. Maybe now, he would stay away forever and just leave her alone.

————

"Are you ready to leave, Dutchy darling?"

Dutchy looked up at Angela as she stood by the bed. "Yes." Oh, she was *so* ready to get out of this place. The sterile smell, the bland food, and the drab surroundings didn't help her mood at all. Not even the dozens of flowers, cards, balloons, and stuffed animals from her friends made the room feel welcoming.

"Let me help you," Angela said.

She hated feeling like an invalid, but that's what she was, wasn't she? Her left arm was in a cast, and she had to wear a sling. Her ribs still hurt when she did anything harder than breathe. Worse, this morning when the nurse came to change her bandages, she caught sight of the surgical wound across the right side of her torso—a long, angry scar held together with stitches. Tears had sprung to her eyes, but the nurse assured her this was normal, and she was healing properly.

No, she wanted to say. This *wasn't* normal. Not for her. She should be fully healed by now. Instead, her body remained weak. Human.

Her fox hissed, as if reminding her of who and why they were in this state. He hadn't even been back in days, not since she told him what happened. *Good*, she told her fox, despite the tightening in her chest.

"Dutchy?"

Her head snapped up to meet Angela's face. She had her hand out, waiting for her to take it. "Uh, yeah. Thanks."

Angela helped her get up from the bed and then walked her over to the door where a nurse strode in with a wheelchair.

"No," Dutchy said adamantly. "I can walk."

"You'll be feeling weak after a few steps, miss," the nurse said. The nameplate on her chest indicated her name was Muriel. "It's normal, seeing as you've been through major surgery and have been in bed for more than a week. You might fall over and hit your head, then we'll have to admit you all over again."

"Dutchy," Angela began. "Please. It's just a short ride to the exit."

"Fine," she grumbled as she sat in the wheelchair. "Let's go."

"It'll be all right, Dutchy." Angela placed a hand on her shoulder. "Your Aunt Rosie and I will take care of you. Your friends, too, promised to help."

"Thank you, Aunt Angela."

Though she hated being coddled like this, she didn't really have much of a choice. The doctor said it might be another month before she could get her cast off. That, plus her surgical wounds and bruised ribs, she couldn't even change her own clothes, much less drive around, and feed and take care of herself.

So, it was decided she would stay with Angela, who lived in a three-bedroom ranch-style house not far from Main Street.

Rosie, Anna Victoria, J.D., and her other friends Kate and Amelia promised to help out when they could.

Muriel rolled her out to the front door, the large glass doors opening automatically as they strolled out together, stopping right at the driveway.

The brisk, autumn air was a soothing balm, and Dutchy was glad to be out of the antiseptic atmosphere of the hospital. She closed her eyes, letting the cool breeze calm her.

"Dutchy."

Her head snapped toward the sound of the voice, and her eyes flew open. Krieger stood six feet away, hands held up. Her fox immediately went on the defensive, arching its back as its ears flattened and bushy tail curled.

"I promise I won't get any closer," he said.

"I thought we told you to leave?" Angela said, her hands planting on her hips. "I don't want her upset."

"I couldn't," he said somberly. "Please. I promised I wouldn't try to get near her again. But I couldn't stay away."

Couldn't stay away? But she had last seen him days ago.

"Dutchy?" Angela's face was marred with concern. Of course, Rosie had already told her everything. "Do you want me to call security?" She met Muriel's gaze, who nodded in acknowledgement.

"I ..." She glanced back at Krieger. Despite her fox's reaction, she couldn't help the way her stomach flip-flopped. "It's all right," she said to the nurse, then turned to Krieger. "What do you want?"

"I just wanted to talk to you." He glanced warily at Angela and the nurse. "Please."

She didn't owe him anything. Her fox, too, didn't want him around. But maybe they could hash this out now and then he'd leave her alone. "Aunt Angela? Muriel? Would you mind?"

Angela hesitated but then said, "All right. I'm going to get the car."

Muriel gestured to the bench next to the door. "I'll be sitting over there," she said before turning on her heel and walking away.

Her aunt gave her a last concerned glance before she, too, strode off in the direction of the parking lot.

"All right then," she said to him when they were alone. "Talk."

His dark brows drew together. "I ... I've had a lot of time to think."

"Yeah, you have." She tried not to sound bitter, but damn it, he was making it so hard. He left her alone, just as she asked. But then, why did it feel like he abandoned her all over again?

"I deserve that." He gritted his teeth. "But you need to know, Dutchy, everything I've done ... the last couple of months ... they've been for you."

"Ha!" Her fox, too, barked sarcastically. "You'll have to excuse me if I don't believe you."

"I've been trying to be better, Dutchy." He fisted his hands at his sides. "I've been working on it. Trying ... trying to be better. For you."

A seething anger bubbled in her. "But why did you push me away in the first place?" God, that day had been months ago, yet it was still so crystal clear in her mind. You need to go back, he had said. *Go.*

"I ... can't explain it exactly."

A pained look flashed across his face, and for a brief second, her gut clenched. "Can't? Or won't?" she spat. When he didn't answer, she laughed bitterly. "I thought so."

"You don't have to ... what I mean is." He took a step forward. "Does it hurt?"

"Hurt?"

He took another step. "Does it hurt you? When I come closer?"

He was about three feet away from her now. She didn't even realize that he'd been inching toward her. "I ... no." Her fox eyed him warily, yes, but it didn't claw at her.

He let out a relieved breath. "Okay."

"Okay, what?"

"Can I come closer?"

She bit her lip. Her fox shook its head. "No."

"But you're not hurting?"

"I said I wasn't," she snapped. "Please, can we just get on with this? What do you want, John?"

"It's my fault you're like this. That you're not healing. And you can't see color. And everything ... everything you said ... I know it now."

"Know what?"

"What I did. I broke you. I broke *us*."

The pang in her heart came unexpectedly. "There is no us."

"I know, and that's my fault." His expression softened, then turned to determination. "And I'm going to fix you."

Was he serious? Her jaw went slack. *He sure sounded and looked serious.* "I don't know if you can."

"I'm going to do it, Dutchy." His hands curled into fists at his sides. "I don't care how long it takes or what I have to do."

"I—"

He moved so quickly; he was practically a blur. She thought he'd disappeared, but she could feel his presence behind her. "I swear to you," he whispered as he leaned down close, though he didn't touch her. "I'm going to fix us."

And with that, he was gone, leaving her heart pounding in her chest.

"Miss?" Muriel asked as she rushed to her side and placed a

hand on her forehead. "Are you all right? You look pale. Should I call the doctor?"

She spied Angela's Ford Focus rounding the corner. "No." She didn't want to go back into the hospital. And if she were honest, her racing pulse had nothing to do with feeling sick.

I'm going to fix us.

Hope threatened to flower in her chest, but she didn't dare nurture it. When he'd first left her that day, she'd daydreamed of something like this. But now, months later, she didn't want to get her hopes up again. He'd already crushed her hopes once and she'd paid for it. She wouldn't be able to survive it a second time.

Chapter 9

A few more days had passed since Krieger saw Dutchy leaving the hospital. While he was glad she was out of there, seeing her looking so frail and vulnerable only drove him and his bear to the brink. He tried to stay away from her initially because he'd been so afraid of hurting her, but found he couldn't, so he went back. Her aunts, however, forbade him from getting near her room, so he waited outside, getting news from Anna Victoria when she came to visit and hoping to catch Dutchy when she was finally discharged

Her fox ... he'd only felt that animosity from his worst enemies. He knew the pain of a broken animal, how his own bear ripped him up from the inside, and he didn't want that happening to her.

It didn't matter that he had worked on himself all these months so he could be good enough for her. He hadn't considered how his actions would affect her. Did he really think that he could just walk away without explanation, then stroll back into her life like nothing had changed? That time had stopped for her, and she would just be waiting in the wings until he was finished making changes to himself?

And he knew, he knew he had to fix her. It was his fault she was broken, so he had to be the one to do it. He fixed himself, so why couldn't he do it for her?

Failure was not an option.

He had to fix her.

But he still didn't know how he was going to go about it.

The knock on the door made him start. "Come in," he said. Not that the person on the other side needed an invitation. After all, only one person came to visit him up here in his cabin.

"Hey," Damon greeted as he strode in.

His former commander entering his cabin reminded him of how he'd started on this path those many months ago.

You know, forgiveness, it's not just something another person has to ask for. Sometimes ... sometimes we have to ask forgiveness of ourselves.

He would never forget those words Damon said to him after he came here to thank him for saving Anna Victoria. That—and the changes he had seen in his friend—was what set off the chain of events that led him to want to change himself, so he could function normally in society and not be trapped here.

"Krieger?"

"Yeah." He blinked away the thousand-yard stare he knew was on his face. "What's up, Chief?"

Damon pulled out a chair, turned it around, and straddled it to face him. "How are you holding up?"

He shrugged. "Same old, same old."

"I came up here to check up on you ... and also, to talk to Milos."

"Milos?" He knew Damon sometimes checked in with his neighbor when Milos's friend couldn't come up. "Is he all right?"

"Yeah. But I wanted to give him a heads-up about Oscar. The raccoon shifter."

Shit. "Sorry, haven't had time to look into it, Chief."

"No, no, I understand, Krieg. I told you to take all the time you need."

"The raccoon hasn't turned up yet?" It had been ... fuck, over two weeks now since that night?

Damon shook his head. "'Fraid not. Then I remembered our wolf friend, so that's why I went to see him. He says he'd be happy to keep an eye out for the raccoon and even patrol the area. God knows, you've earned any time off you want. Just give him a heads-up if you need to be away."

His bear chuffed as it considered this area their territory to guard, but then again, that would give him time to figure stuff out with Dutchy. "Thanks, Chief."

"So, Anna Victoria's out with the girls tonight. Do you wanna come down and get a drink at The Den with me? I could use the company."

His first instinct was to say no, but the fact that Damon was the one asking to come out to a crowded place was a big deal. "Sure thing, Chief."

"Good, let's go."

The trip down from his cabin to town was a long one, but both of them sat in comfortable silence. Or perhaps, they were girding themselves for the noise and crowd they were about to face since it was a Friday night. As they entered The Den, Tim signaled to them and nodded to the private room in the back. When they got there, he was surprised that there were three other men already waiting in the lone occupied table.

"You're here," Gabriel Russel greeted.

"Chief. Krieger." Daniel Rogers raised his beer to them.

"Finally." Anders Stevens rolled his eyes.

Something about this whole thing felt like a set-up. "What's this about?" he asked Damon, crossing his arms over his chest.

"Relax, Krieger," Damon began. "When was the last time all of us were together? Over five years ago? Back in training?"

"Yeah, the year of hell," Gabriel groaned.

"You're still salty because Simpson wouldn't let you keep your hairdryer in the barracks?" Anders said.

Daniel was in the middle of sipping from his beer when he snorted, then choked, sending a spray of liquid forward.

"Dude!" Anders jumped back.

"S-sorry!" Daniel wiped his nose with a napkin. "I was just thinking about that first hike we went on and that bat got caught in Gabriel's hair and he had to cut two inches off of it."

Everyone except Gabriel burst out laughing, and even Krieger couldn't stop himself from smiling.

"Fine, be that way," Gabriel grumbled as he sipped from his glass, though the corners of his mouth tugged up.

"I thought it was time we all got together again," Damon said. "And I think we could all use some good news."

"Hell yeah!" Anders slammed a palm down on the table. "I'm glad you asked us to come, Chief, because you all should be the first to know—you're now looking at a mated man."

So, Anders finally bonded with his mate. Envy stabbed through Krieger's chest, but he said nothing. Anders had been in a terrible state right after they rescued his mate from her kidnappers, so he was glad they worked it out.

Daniel glowered at the tiger shifter. "Oh, I already know all right. You really should put on some pants when you answer the door in *my* house."

"You were cramping my style, Rogers," Anders shot back. "Or should I start calling you 'bro' now? When can I move in?"

The bear shifter groaned and slapped his palm on his forehead.

"I'm kidding, I'm kidding." Anders laughed aloud and slapped him on the shoulder. "Besides, though your

McMansion's pretty big, it's gonna get pretty crowded once the baby—" All of a sudden, blood drained from Anders's face, and his arms fell down to his sides. "*Fuck.*"

"Anders?" Gabriel waved a hand in front of the tiger shifter's face. "You all right?"

His jaw dropped. "I'm gonna be a *dad.*" He grabbed his glass and knocked back the contents. "Guys, I'm gonna be a dad!" he shouted, as if he had just realized it now.

Gabriel and Damon slapped him on the shoulders and congratulated him. Daniel stood back, looking smug as he obviously already knew.

"Congratulations," Krieger said and offered his hand.

"Thanks, man." Anders shook it vigorously.

There was something about Anders ... a different air to him that Krieger could not quite put his finger on. In his previous encounters with the tiger shifter, there had been a simmering anger bubbling there, a chip on his shoulder that was permanently buried there. But now ... he couldn't describe it accurately, but there was an underlying peace under the tiger shifter's boisterous demeanor. Was this what it was like to be bonded and mated? The envy twitched inside him once again.

"And really, thank you." Anders continued. "If it wasn't for you ... I don't even know if she would ..."

"Are you crying, Stevens?" Gabriel asked incredulously.

"No!" Anders denied as he cleared his throat. "What the fuck are you talking about?"

Damon sighed. "All right, all right." His lips quirked up. "Now, that wasn't exactly what I meant when I mentioned good news, but I'll forgive you this time for showing me up with *your* news before I could share mine." There was a twinkle in the chief's eyes that Krieger had just noticed.

"Showing you up—" Gabriel's eyes widened. "No. Really?"

A rare smile broke out from the chief. "Really. We're having a baby. Anna Victoria's out with the girls to tell them tonight."

"Oh man!" Gabriel engulfed him in a hug. "Damon ... I'm so happy for you guys!"

"Here, here." Daniel raised his beer bottle. "Congrats, Chief."

"Fuck yeah!" Anders clinked his glass to Daniel's bottle, then slapped Damon on the back once Gabriel released him. "Hey, we're gonna be dads! Let me get everyone a drink. What do you want, Daddy?" he asked Damon, then winced. "Wait, that didn't come out the way I wanted it to."

To his credit, Damon barked out a chuckle. "A beer would be fine."

"And you, Krieger?"

It took him a second to answer. "Same."

"All right." Anders gave them a thumbs-up before he strode out to the bar.

"You okay, Krieg?" Damon asked.

"Congratulations, Chief. To both of you." Envy twisted deeper in his chest, but he managed to swallow it like a bitter pill.

"Thanks. I'm glad you came down here so I could give everyone the news at the same time. Anna Victoria took a home pregnancy test a couple days ago and we confirmed it at the doctor's office today."

"When's she due?" Gabriel asked.

"Late April." Damon now, too, had the same look of panic Anders had earlier. "Geez. A baby. I mean ... we decide to try, and she stopped taking her birth control as soon as they ran out, but ... I didn't think it would be quite this soon."

"Hey, it'll be fine, Damon," Gabriel assured him. "We're here for you."

"Yeah, whatever you need, Chief," Daniel added. "Right, Krieg?"

"Of course." That, at least, he could be sure of. He would protect these men and theirs with his very last breath.

"Here you go guys," Anders said as he came back, carrying four mugs of frothy, ice-cold beer, and handed one to each of the men around the table. "Again, congrats, Chief."

"Same to you." Damon grabbed one of the mugs and raised it. They all followed suit and clinked their glasses together. Damon cleared his throat. "There's one more thing."

Once those words were spoken, all four gazes zeroed in on Krieger. For the first time in his life, he suddenly felt like prey. "What the hell is goin' on?" he growled. It seemed his earlier suspicion about this being a set up wasn't unwarranted.

"Krieg," Damon began. "It's not what you think. Please, stand down."

"We wanna help," Anders continued.

"Like you've helped us," Gabriel added, and Daniel concurred with a nod of his head.

"Help you?"

"Don't think we haven't noticed," Gabriel said. "You've been watching over us these past months. You took out that asshole who nearly burned Temperance."

"And you helped me when those anti-shifters caught me," Daniel reminded him.

"Like I said, if you hadn't been there, that bastard would have hurt Darcey," Anders added.

"I wasn't doing it for you," he huffed.

"We know," Anders said somberly. "You were trying to be a better man. For her, right?"

"And we understand," Damon said. "I do, most of all. So, let us help you."

Though he had not seen a lot of these men in the last five

years, that one year of training they had all gone through together had forged a bond between them that could never be broken. Each of them had made a mark on him in their own way. Damon had been the one to bring him here, despite the state he was in. Gabriel was the first to reach out and try to befriend him even though his efforts didn't prove fruitful. Daniel never judged him or pried too much, but rather, had been a silent source of strength and inspiration. And in Anders —the real Anders, not the one he made himself out to be— Krieger had seen a good heart, despite his inner and external struggles.

It was Damon who broke the silence. "What can we do, Krieg? To help you win your mate?"

"I ... I don't know if you can help me. If anyone can help me." And because he trusted these men, and they trusted him back, he told them everything. "... I know. I'm the bastard who left her. I just ... I didn't know it would end up like this. If only I went to her right after I realized ... and I didn't wait—"

"Shoulda, woulda, coulda." Gabriel shook his head. "You can't do anything about the past. You can only decide on what you want to do now."

"But what?" He raked his fingers through his scalp. "I've been racking my brains out tryin' to find a way to fix her."

"Hmmm." Anders rubbed his chin with his thumb and forefinger. "What do you know about her?"

"Excuse me?"

"You know ... what does she like? Dislike? Hobbies, favorite movies, stuff like that?"

"Uh ... I don't know."

"You don't know?" Anders asked. "I thought you spent all that time alone with her?"

"Yeah, but ... we didn't do much talking."

For the second time that night, Daniel sprayed beer through his nose.

"Jesus, Rogers, if you can't hold your drink ..." Anders tsked, then turned to Krieger. "Sarge, you dog!" he chuckled. "I knew the rumors about you weren't an exaggeration."

Not wanting to go *there*, Krieger said, "But why are you asking me about her hobbies?" Dutchy designed clothes, that was all he knew about her.

"You gotta woo her," Anders said. "And win her over with things she likes."

"Like with flowers and shit?" He gnawed at his inner cheek. "I don't think that's gonna cut it."

"The bond hasn't formed yet, right?" Daniel asked.

"No." He was at least sure of that.

"Maybe that's the solution there," Anders said. "Claim and bond her, then everything will work out."

Would that really work? "But how do I do that?"

Daniel scratched his head. "Hold up. To fix her, you need to bond with her, and in order for that to happen, you both need to be open to it. To want it and each other, without any barriers."

"But if you're saying she won't even let you near her," Gabriel continued. "Then how can you even form the mating bond?"

Now he was confused. "Well, what should I do now? How did you all claim and bond with your mates?"

No one said a word, but they all looked at each other. Krieger rapped his fingers on the table impatiently until finally, Damon spoke up. "I think ... I think everyone had some good ideas. But Dutchy is her own person, and there are going to be some things that might have worked for us that might not work for you."

"I thought you were here to help me," he snapped, then quickly added, "Sorry. I just ... I don't know what to do."

"Hey, it's all right man, we've all been there," Gabriel placed a tentative hand on his shoulder. "And ... well I can't believe I'm saying this, but what Anders said has some merit."

"Oh, ha ha, thanks rich boy," Anders said sarcastically.

Gabriel shot him a glare, then turned back to Krieger. "If you don't know her, then maybe it's time to get to know who she is. Get to know the real her and figure out why she's broken. You can't fix something if you don't know why it's broke."

"It's because of me," he said adamantly. "*I* broke her. And she hates me."

"She doesn't hate you," Daniel said. "And neither does her fox."

"You don't understand—"

"Besides, even if she did, it's not the worst thing," Gabriel added. "Hate isn't the opposite of love, you know. It's indifference."

"She's just mad and hurt," Anders pointed out. "And it's understandable. Rejection is hard to get over."

"I didn't reject her ... well, I did at first. Fuck, why didn't I see it?" He gnashed his teeth together. That day he told her to go. No, he didn't just do that. He left her on the side of the mountain. "You're right." But where to begin?

"You guys must have talked *some*, right?" Anders said. "Even a little."

"Yeah." Of course they did. Every single thing Dutchy said in that short span of time was burned into his mind. How could he forget?

"Also, sometimes it's not about what a woman says or does." Gabriel said. "It's about what she doesn't say."

"What—" Gabriel's words gave him an idea. Actually, everything they all said was beginning to make sense now. It was time he fully got to know who Dutchy was, and from there, figure out how he was going to heal her.

Breaking and entering into her home was probably not the best way to get to know Dutchy, but he would do anything to get her back. Damon knew where it was as Dutchy had designed Anna Victoria's gown, and he'd picked her up there once. So, before Krieger went back to his cabin, he decided to stop by for a visit.

The small, single-story home was located just at the edge of town. It looked ordinary enough, painted blue and white with a small lawn outside that sadly had seen better days. He crept around to the backyard and approached the back door. Jiggling it experimentally, he applied his shifter strength and broke the handle, then pulled it open.

The first thing that hit him was the powerful stench of garbage. *Jesus.* Well, it had been two weeks since she was home, so her trash was probably just sitting inside, rotting in the bin. Still, the pile of dishes in the sink, boxes of takeout containers on the table, and growing stack of mail on the counter looked like they had been weeks old.

Striding out of the kitchen, he walked down the narrow hallway. The first door he passed by was ajar, so he peeked inside. From the scent in the air, he knew it was her bedroom, and he stepped inside.

The queen-sized bed was unmade, and clothes were left in a pile in the corner, but it wasn't in as bad a state as the kitchen. Before leaving, he reached for the silk robe hanging from a hook behind the door and pressed it to his nose. *Dutchy.* Her scent had long faded from his uniform shirt and his sheets, but he would sometimes imagine it was still there, only the memory of it burned in his mind.

Forcing himself to leave her most private den, he continued his exploration of her house, glad to see that at least the living room looked in order. It was homey, not overly feminine, but comfortable and lived-in, for sure. One wall held a shelf of books. Half were big glossy coffee table books about fashion and photography, but the rest were novels. He pulled one out, noting the well-worn spine, and raised a brow at the cover featuring a man clad in nothing but a kilt, well-built chest bared, holding a woman whose breasts threatened to spill out of her top. He put it back and did a cursory scan of the other spines noting the titles and author names. All romance novels, a fact he filed away in his brain before turning to inspect the rest of the room.

There were various photos and knickknacks on the wall. Pictures of her with friends. Parties. Weddings. But the one of her wearing a graduation cap and a red robe, her arms around an older woman, caught his eye. The woman looked so much like Dutchy that he concluded it was probably her mother.

He was about to turn back when he saw another door on the other side of the living room, so he approached it. It was closed, but not locked, so he pushed it open.

Stepping inside, he deduced this was her work space. Two sewing machines were pushed against one of the windows. Several bolts of fabric were propped up against the corner while three torso mannequins stood like soldiers along one wall. Two were completely bare, a pool of fabric at the foot, as if they had been hastily torn off. The last mannequin's dress was barely clinging on with one of its shoulders ripped down. Pinned up on the wall behind it was what looked like an illustration of the same dress. Or half of an illustration anyway. It was torn, ripped down the middle. Taking the corner hanging down, he pushed it up, the jagged edges meeting perfectly to form a whole picture.

Krieger wasn't a fashion expert by any means, but his breath caught at the beauty of the work—the colors, the masterful strokes of the pen, and the sheer talent it took to transform pen and ink into something real. The gown on the mannequin looked like dragonfly wings layered across the torso, the gorgeous blue and green iridescent fabric like gossamer, fanning out into a full skirt. It didn't really hit him until now how talented his mate was and how humble she had been. To say she only designed gowns was like saying Michelangelo only painted ceilings.

Walking past the mannequins, he padded over to the large wooden desk next to a drafting table. There was a lamp and a laptop computer, and a magazine that was left open on a spread with a beautiful woman wearing a stunning bronze and gold gown as she stood atop a grand staircase. "Royal Wedding of the Century" the headline proclaimed. But he didn't bother reading the article, because what caught his eye was the photo inset at the bottom right. It was of Dutchy, wearing a pale blue gown, on the arm of a handsome, dark-haired man in a black doublet and kilt. The caption underneath read, *Gown designer and bridesmaid Duchess Forrester with groomsman Ian MacGregor, Duke of Rothschilde.*

He wanted to tear that page out and shred it to a million pieces with his claws. His bear agreed, but he reined it in. This magazine was obviously important to Dutchy, and though he hated seeing her next to another male, he had to remind himself it was only a photo.

Closing the magazine, he turned to her drafting table, but nearly tripped over the several dozen colored pencils, markers, and brushes scattered across the floor, as if someone had tipped over a container full of them and forgot to clean up. On top of the table was a large ring bound sketchbook. Unable to stop himself, he flipped the top open.

The front page was clean, as was the one after it. Strange, as the torn pieces still stuck on the ring indicated this wasn't a new sketchbook. As he shuffled closer to inspect the table, he kicked at something. Bending down, he picked up a balled-up piece of paper. And another. Inspecting the underside of her table, he found several more, made from the same heavy-duty stock as the sketchbook.

He gathered about a dozen of them, finding more underneath her oak desk and unfolded each one, frowning as he saw what was on them. Half-finished sketches. Some just had naked figures. Others were wavy lines and colored pencil strokes. His eyes darted back to the empty sketchbook, noting the layer of dust he didn't notice before on the drafting table and the art supplies.

When she had told him that she couldn't work and couldn't see color, it had been an abstract idea. But now, seeing her gowns across the room and the pages of scrawls, unfinished sketches, and empty pages, it struck him like lightning. He was seeing her devolve. This was what she meant when she said she couldn't work or see color.

This was how broken she was.

He balled up one of the pages and grit his teeth. Her work, her talent—he couldn't let it disappear. But surely, it didn't just evaporate into thin air. No, this ability was innate in Dutchy, carefully cultivated with years of hard work, even before they met. She had it in her, he knew it. He wasn't just going to stand by and let her brilliance be extinguished, not because of a mistake he'd made.

Her world was turning drab, gray, and lifeless? Well then, it was up to him to show her the colors again.

Chapter 10

"Anything else I can get you?" J.D. McNamara asked as she sat down on the sectional sofa in Angela's living room.

"I'm fine," Dutchy said, scratching at her cast. "Thanks for coming over again. Sorry to bother you."

J.D., Anna Victoria, and her other friends had been taking turns coming over every morning to help her clean up, dress, and prepare her some food for the day until Angela arrived after work.

"Dutch—"

"I know you're busy at work," she interrupted. J.D.'s phone hadn't stopped ringing since she arrived, and from the snippets of conversation she heard, it sounded like they were in the weeds back in her garage.

"One of my guys has gone AWOL," she said, a frown marring her pretty face. "No one's seen the old birdbrain in days. But ... that's nothing you need to concern yourself about. I can handle it. And I told you, it's no bother, Dutch." The blonde mechanic plopped herself down across from her. "We promised we'd take good care of you. You scared us, you know."

Her gaze dropped down to her lap. "I don't know if I

deserve that, after how I've been acting the last few months. Flaking out on plans. Ignoring calls and messages. Not to mention, I almost ruined Anna Victoria's wedding—"

"Stop it." J.D. held a hand up. "You didn't ruin anything. The wedding pushed through; you were just a little late."

Actually, she had been a few hours late. She was supposed to be at J.D.'s place at nine the morning of the wedding to deliver the wedding dress, but she'd slept through her alarm. When she woke up at eleven, she had a ton of missed calls from J.D., Anna Victoria, and her other friends. She raced to get to them on time, but she hadn't finished making the adjustments she was supposed to do since the last fitting, so it took another couple of hours for her to hand sew everything.

"How are you feeling?" J.D. asked.

"Okay, I guess." It was the same answer she gave every time anyone asked her. Her body was healing, but at a glacially slow pace. Her arm and shoulder felt stiff, her ribs still stung when she overexerted herself, and doing something as simple as going to the bathroom left her exhausted. *At least the stitches had come out.* The puckered scar on her torso was a reminder of her weakness and her current state. *Why?* she asked her vixen. *Why are you doing this?* But no matter how many times she asked, it wouldn't answer her.

"No, no, no." Tendrils of messy blonde hair escaped from under the trucker hat as J.D. shook her head vehemently. "I mean, how are *you* feeling? And don't give me these bullshit answers, Dutch. I know something's wrong."

Her head snapped up to meet luminous light hazel eyes. Being a shifter, J.D. could read her and her fox and could probably sense there was something not quite right.

The loud and boisterous tomboy hadn't been one of her original friends when she moved to Blackstone, but the two of them had been roped into many a girls' night with Sybil, Kate,

Amelia, and the rest of their close-knit family. Being the only two single girls, they had gravitated toward each other, especially when everyone became busy with their lives.

"I just—" A knock on the door saved her from having to evade the question or outright lie to her friend.

J.D. blew a breath out. "I'll go see who that is."

"Thanks," she said, relief pouring through her. Her ribs were starting to hurt again, so she leaned back and closed her eyes. Her hearing could pick up the sounds of J.D. opening the door, talking to someone, and then shutting the door.

"Who is it?" she asked.

"Delivery." J.D. held up a small box wrapped in brown paper. "You expecting something?"

"No."

J.D. set the package on her lap gently. "Is there a card?"

"Doesn't seem to be one." Curious, she tore away the packaging, then opened the box and peered inside. *Huh?*

"What is it?"

She took out the object from within—a glass snow globe, the size of a grapefruit. Holding it up, she waited for the white flakes to settle, revealing a small log cabin nestled between pine trees covered in snow. Her heart skipped a beat.

"A snow globe?" J.D. wrinkled her nose. "Who is it from?"

She knew who it was from, of course. But why send this?

"It's from him, right?" the mechanic said smugly. "I can tell from the look on your face. It's true then? That guy ... is your mate?"

Not like she could lie now. "How did you guess?"

"It's obvious. At least, Anna Victoria said so. The way he wouldn't leave you while you were recovering from surgery. Even when you woke up and threw him out, he hung around the hospital every day. When Anna Victoria and I came to visit, he would ask us how you were doing."

"And you told him?"

"No, no. Not like that. He just wanted to make sure you were okay. What happened?" J.D. continued. "With you and Krieger?"

Her fox hissed at the mention of the name, and her gaze dropped back to the snow globe. What was this about? He was obviously trying to remind her of their short time together. A little flare of heat sparked in her core at the reminder of those two nights they spent wrapped up in each other's arms. The feel of him on top of her. His hard body and—

"You all right, Dutch?" J.D. peered at her curiously.

"Um. Yeah." She shoved the snow globe back in the box. "I'm fine." But what was Krieger up to?

The following day, another package arrived, this time in the form of a food delivery—toast, and bacon and eggs from the local diner. *Like the breakfast he made.* The meal itself hadn't been memorable, but what they'd done on that table after sure was.

In the next few days, more gifts came to her aunt's doorstep. He sent her a basket of bath bombs, salts, and candles. She smiled, thinking about how she had told him she loved long baths. Then a teddy bear wearing a Blackstone Rangers uniform shirt, similar to his uniform that she wore around the cabin.

The gifts didn't stop with just her, either. No, Krieger sent flowers to both her aunts. And Rosie said he stopped by to eat at the pie shop, devouring an entire pie by himself—cherry with extra whipped cream.

It had been so long ago ... how did he remember such details in their brief time together? What was he trying to say?

A few more packages and food deliveries came in the following week. Takeout from her favorite Chinese place. Pizza from Giorgio's, the local Italian restaurant. Greek food from a new restaurant on Main Street. Thai food from the food court in

South Blackstone. She and Angela didn't have to cook for the next two weeks as lunches and dinners would just magically show up on their doorstep.

Then one day, the strangest gift of all arrived—a box of romance novels, delivered by Isla, who introduced herself as the owner of the local bookshop that had just opened up on Main Street. She couldn't stop from smiling when the bespectacled young woman told her that a huge scary man came in asking for all her latest romance titles, except anything where the man on the cover wears a kilt.

What are you up to, Krieger?

And more important, where was he?

It had been over three weeks since she'd seen him outside the hospital. Her vixen did not like her train of thought. In fact, it didn't like any of the gifts. But Dutchy couldn't stop the butterflies in her stomach from fluttering or her heart hammering in anticipation as she waited and wondered what the day's gift would be.

So, when the doorbell rang the next afternoon, she raced to the front door—well, walked briskly anyway, as even though she was feeling better, her arm and shoulder were still sore.

She yanked the door open, expecting a deliveryman on the other side. However, her heart slammed into her rib cage as she stared up at the man himself.

From the look on his face, he wasn't expecting to see her up close either. "I—" He took a few steps back from the door. "Is this okay?"

For a moment, she was distracted by his presence and aura. The dark T-shirt he wore stretched over his powerful shoulders, molding to them like they'd been painted on. "Huh?

"Am I far away enough?"

"Oh." He was still concerned about her fox hurting her. "Yes, it's fine." Funny enough, though her animal seethed at the sight of him, his presence didn't trigger any violent reactions. "Um, thank you for the gifts."

"You got them all?"

"Yeah." She bit her lip as she shuffled her feet. "I don't get it though." Slowly, she lifted her head to meet his gaze. Her heart ached, wishing she could see that indescribable blue of his eyes again. "Why?"

He paused. "I told you why."

I'm going to fix you. I'm going to fix us.

Those words haunted her every day, lurking in the back of her mind. Yet, she didn't know how the gifts fit in except to remind her of what they'd shared in the past. Her fox yipped in protest, reminding her that that's all it was—things that happened in the past. *He left you on the side of that mountain. Tossed you aside like you meant nothing and now—*

"Will you come with me?"

"What?"

He jerked his thumb behind him toward a pickup truck sitting in the driveway. "I'd like to take you out."

"Out?"

"For a drive, that's all," he said. "You must be bored, being cooped up inside. But only if your animal isn't hurting you."

His concern for her and her animal caught her off guard. The vixen too, paused in its protest. "No. I mean it's not ... so, yes." Oh God, did she really say yes? *I should tell him no.*

"Really?" An elated, boyish expression briefly crossed his face, and she realized she couldn't take it back now. "Thank you."

"Let me get my purse and coat." Turning on her heel, she headed to the living room and typed out a brief text message to Angela, explaining that she was going out with a friend, but not specifying who. This whole bizarre turn of events was hard to explain, even to herself. But anticipation thrummed in her veins as she headed back to the door. Maybe it was just the excitement of actually being able to leave the house. "Okay, I'm ready."

"Let's go."

He led her toward the pickup truck and held the door open, but kept his distance and didn't try to touch her. Circling to the driver's side, he slid in carefully, watching her reaction. "Are you ... is your fox ..."

Her animal curled its tail and flattened its ears defensively, but Dutchy ignored the warnings. "Yes. It's fine."

His shoulders relaxed and he grabbed the seatbelt, strapped himself in, then started the engine. "Just let me know if you're uncomfortable or you're hurting. We'll stop. I'll take you back."

She didn't answer, but he didn't seem to mind as he kept his eye on the road and drove off.

Oh God, what am I doing here? This was crazy, right? She was supposed to hate him. Her fox hated him. Even now, its back was arched and ears flattened, waiting for Krieger to make a wrong move.

"Where are we going?" she finally thought to ask. They had been driving for half an hour now, and she didn't recognize the road they were taking.

"I thought ... maybe you'd like to see the mountains."

"The m-mountains?"

He nodded. "There are roads and trails closed off to the public, even to shifters, that only rangers can access. But where I'm taking you ... you don't need to get out of the car."

The pickup veered up to an unpaved trail, ending at an enclosed gate with a sign that read "Private Property, Keep Out." However, a guard's head emerged from the security shack. When he spotted Krieger in the driver's seat, he waved as the gates opened.

They lumbered through the rough gravel paved roads and

after a few minutes, they turned a corner, stopping at a flat, scenic viewpoint that overlooked a giant lake.

"Oh." The view was breathtaking, and she immediately recognized the place. Aside from the castle and its grounds, it was one of the areas in the mountains the Lennoxes kept as private property. Sybil and Amelia had invited her to their parents' cabins there several times.

"You've been here before?" he asked.

"At the lake, yes. But I've never seen it from up here." The water was so calm that a clear mirror image reflection of the mountains appeared on its surface.

"I've been coming here a lot," he confessed. "Sometimes I see the dragons fly overhead."

"Must be a sight." She had to admit, even though she was friends with Sybil Lennox, she had never seen her or anyone in her family in dragon form before. "But why did you bring me here?"

His gaze remained fixed on the lake. "This is where I go when I need to get my head on straight. I ... I grew up just outside Duluth, near Lake Superior. This place reminds me of that."

"Is your family still there?"

"Yeah. My parents and my sister. Grandma and Grandpa. My brothers are all over though."

He has family. Of course he does. Curiosity got the better of her. "And you go to visit a lot?"

He stiffened. "Not really. I call and email sometimes. Just to keep updated. Let them know I'm okay and to check on them."

"You should go visit them. Maybe for the holidays," she suggested. "I haven't been home to my skulk for almost a year and a half now."

"Connecticut, right?"

Her head swung back to him. "You were listening to me babbling on and on?"

"Of course." He met her gaze. "I heard every word you said. Remembered everything about you. How could I forget?"

Her heart drummed with excitement as a flash of heat spread down her spine. She tamped it down, the feelings raw and frightening. "Th-thank you for taking me here. It's beautiful."

"In the winter, Lake Superior gets covered in snow. And you know when we say covered snow up there, we mean *covered*. It's the lake effect—cold air picks up the warmer air from the lake and blows it across the shores. And when that happens, everything is white. The water's just this dark gray color, and even the cliffs get covered in ice. You'd think ... you'd think it was sad because you can't see the clear waters or the trees. But it's actually quite stunning."

She had closed her eyes as he was describing his home, his voice lulling her. It was probably the most he'd ever said to her in one breath, and the way he described it, she could picture it in her mind. The snow forming over the edges of the gray water. Icicles clinging to rock faces. "It sounds amazing."

"It is," he said.

They stayed there for a few more minutes, a comfortable silence resting over them. "I can take you back, if you like," he said.

Unsure what to say, she nodded, and he started the engine. The rest of the ride was a blur and soon they were pulling up in front of Angela's house. When she reached for the door, he spoke.

"Can I see you again tomorrow?"

She froze for a second, then turned her head to meet his gaze, startled as he was looking at her head on. For a moment she thought ... no, she was imagining things. "Tomorrow?"

"Yeah. I spoke to Rosie yesterday. She says she misses you and feels bad she hasn't been around to see you in days."

"Ah. Right." One of Rosie's waitresses quit without warning and she'd been covering for her.

"How about I drive you there for lunch? She'd love to see you."

"*She'd* like to see me?"

"Yeah." His Adam's apple bobbed up and down. "And ... I would too."

"All right." When his face lit up, her body tensed, and a dizzy feeling came over her.

What the—

There it was again. Her stomach flip-flopped. But was she seeing things, or did it really happen?

"Dutchy?" He cocked his head at her. "You okay?"

"Uh-huh," she stammered and looked away, her face feeling hot. "Um, I should go."

"I'll come by at eleven-thirty."

Not bothering to respond, she darted out of the truck and made a beeline for the door. It was a miracle she made it all the way inside as her knees wobbled through the entire short sprint, and it wasn't because she was fatigued.

Leaning against the door behind her, she pressed a hand to her chest.

Oh Lord. What was she thinking? Well, she wasn't. Her fox, too, admonished her for accepting his invitation. Yet ... her heart soared at the thought of seeing him again.

And what she'd seen ... she thought it was her imagination, but then it happened again. It was brief, like the failed spark from a lighter.

A flash of bright blue from the depths of his gaze.

But the idea of it being real scared her. And why? She didn't know.

Chapter 11

Krieger had never cared much for his appearance in the last five years he'd lived here. Back when before he'd been deployed and lived on the base, he and his army buddies would get all dressed up on weekend nights before they hit the bars in search of some fun.

However, living by himself up in the mountains, there had been no point in shaving, cutting his hair, or even buying new clothes. But now he wished he at least had some proper scissors and a razor to trim his beard. Or a shirt that wasn't faded or full of holes. To someone like Dutchy, he probably looked like some hobo mountain man. Not knowing what to do, he went to the one person he could run to for help.

"Er, I'm not much of clothes expert either," Damon said. He had driven down from his cabin in the truck Gabriel had lent him to Damon's place. The chief also lived in the mountains, but lower down from him in one of the few areas the Lennoxes leased lands for rangers. "I know someone who is. Anna Victoria."

The chief's mate was more than happy to help when

Damon called her down and explained the situation. "Ooh! Shopping trip," she exclaimed, clapping her hands together.

"Anna Victoria," Damon warned. "Don't go overboard, now."

She laughed. "I won't, I promise. And I know just the place. Let me go get my keys, and we can head out."

Soon, Krieger found himself in South Blackstone, one of the newer developments in town that had lots of boutiques, restaurants, and cafes. It was strange to spend time with Anna Victoria without Damon, but she seemed determined to get him some new clothes. She led him to a men's boutique, which because they had just opened, was empty save for the salesperson inside who greeted them as they entered.

"I don't have much time," Krieger said as he glanced up at the clock hanging over the counter. It was already nine thirty-five. "Also, I don't know where to start." The rows of shirts, jackets, and pants around him looked ... intimidating.

"We won't take long." Anna Victoria pushed him into the dressing room. "And I'll take care of it, okay?"

Forty-five minutes later, they left the store with two bags, plus he was wearing a new outfit—white shirt, black leather jacket, and new jeans. "Are you sure this is okay?"

Anna Victoria's smile was as wide as the ocean. "It's more than okay. She'll *love* it."

It didn't surprise him that she knew why he wanted to get some new clothes. "What about this?" He grabbed a handful of his unruly hair. "Should I cut it off?"

"No!" The female sounded like she was going to have a heart attack at the mere suggestion. "I mean ... you just need a little grooming. C'mon, I know another place we should go to."

Just a few shops down from the men's boutique was a hair salon. He stopped short, seeing the pink and yellow decor from the outside. "I don't think—"

"Don't be a baby, Krieger," Anna Victoria teased. "Trust me, okay? C'mon."

The woman at the front desk introduced herself as Amy, the owner of the salon. From the way she and Anna Victoria chatted, it was obvious they were friends.

"His hair just needs a little TLC," Anna Victoria explained. "Nothing fancy. He has to pick up his date in an hour."

Amy raised a brow at him. "I'm digging the hipster mountain man look, but I bet that hair of yours has got more split ends than my relationship history," she chuckled. "C'mon, honey, I'll take good care of you." She winked at him and led him to the washing basin in the back.

An hour later, Amy had given him a shampoo, trim, and blow-dry, plus also groomed his beard hair. She showed him how to put his hair up in a "man bun" which she said would "drive the ladies wild." Frankly, it seemed strange to go through all that trouble to fix up his hair only to tie it up again in a messy bun, but he shrugged and left it up anyway.

"You look great," Anna Victoria said as they walked out of the salon.

"Thanks ... for everything," he said gratefully. "I gotta go ..."

"Of course." She waved him away. "Now, go knock her socks off!"

Thankfully, he was only five minutes late by the time he pulled up in front of Angela's house. He sprinted to the front door and rang the bell. The door opened seconds later.

"You're"—Dutchy's eyes widened comically as her gaze ran over him from head to toe—"late."

"I'm sorry." He didn't miss the flash of heat in her eyes, and he knew he owed Anna Victoria. *Big time.* "I got held up."

She cleared her throat. "Uh, you look ... nice."

"So do you." Of course, Dutchy always looked amazing, whether she was wearing sweats like yesterday or his uniform shirt. *Or nothing at all*, he added silently. Today, however, she wore a pale blue sweater that matched her eyes, and her brilliant coppery hair fell in waves around her face and down her shoulders. "Beautiful, actually."

"Th-thanks. Angela helped." She gestured to her left arm which was still in a cast, but he was glad to see she no longer needed the sling today. "Should we go? Rosie was excited to hear we were coming."

"Of course."

He led her to the truck and opened the door for her, and soon they were pulling in front of Rosie's Bakery and Cafe. As soon as they came in, Rosie's face lit up from across the room where she was pouring coffee for a two-top. "I'll be right with you, just a sec!" she called to a table as she breezed past them to get to Dutchy and Krieger. "My dear girl." She pulled Dutchy into a hug. "It's so nice to see you out and about." An auburn brow shot up at Krieger. "Oh my ... I almost didn't recognize you. Don't you look handsome?" she said with a saucy wink.

"Uh—"

"Aunt Rosie, do you have a table for us?" Dutchy interrupted.

"Of course. I reserved you your favorite booth."

Rosie led them to a booth right by a large window that had a view of the street. Dutchy slid into the seat facing the dining room, and he sat opposite of her. "Sorry," she cocked her head at the other tables. "I should see to a couple of tables. But Gabriel will be right with you," she said with a wave as she rushed off.

Dutchy's brows drew together. "Gabriel?"

As if on cue, the former ranger came up to them. "Hey folks, what can I—oh, Sarge!" The lion shifter slapped him on the back. "Looking good, man! You sure clean up nice. Love the hair." He shook his own dark golden locks. "Maybe if you keep this up, you'll have hair as nice as mine."

Krieger grumbled. "Can we order?"

He barked out a laugh and turned to Dutchy. "Hello, you must be Dutchy. Gabriel Russel, at your service." He held out a hand.

She took it. "I didn't realize Aunt Rosie had hired someone to replace Bridgette."

"Well, not quite. I'm still learning the ropes, seeing as I'm buying out Rosie. My fiancée, Temperance, has been running the kitchen for a while now, and so we're gonna take over once Rosie feels ready to step back."

"B-b-buying her out?" Dutchy's jaw dropped, and her face went pale.

It was obvious she had no idea what her aunt had planned. Not liking to see her upset, Krieger turned to Gabriel. "Can you give us a minute?"

"Sure. Let me get you some coffee, and I'll come back to let you know the specials."

As soon as Gabriel was out of earshot, he turned to Dutchy. "You didn't know?"

Her gaze dropped down to her lap. "No."

"Gabriel's a good guy," he assured her. "He'll take care of this place. And his mate's an amazing baker. They'll treat Rosie's with respect."

"It's not that," she said in a quiet voice. "I just ... I'm happy for Rosie. God knows she's earned the right to put her feet up and lie back on a beach all day. But I literally had no idea she was retiring until now, because I've been staying away from my aunts and all my friends. Who knows what else I missed while I've been wallowing in pity because I can't get any stupid work done? I'm a terrible person."

"Don't talk like that." He wished he could reach out and embrace her. Hell, he'd settle on holding her hand. But it was too risky. "Rosie doesn't seem like the type to hold a grudge. She obviously loves you."

"And Gabriel ... Oh God." She slapped a palm on her forehead. "He's *the* Gabriel Russel. Only male heir to the Lyon Industries fortune. His fiancée and their wedding planner called me a couple of times about designing her gown, and I didn't even bother to answer. I'll never get another client again."

"Do you need money?" he asked quickly. He wasn't sure how much he had in the bank, but after cashing out his pension and barely spending a dime of his salary in the last five years, it had to be substantial. "I can give you—"

"No, no, it's not that." Her teeth worried at her lip. "I'm all right, I still have my savings that will see me through for another year even if I don't work. It's more about my reputation. People will think I'm a flake. I mean ... I *am* a flake. So maybe I don't deserve a career in fashion."

His chest tightened. "Don't be too hard on yourself." His bear growled, as if reminding him why she was in this state. *Yeah, I know.* But this was why he was trying to fix her. "Gabriel's easygoing. He won't hold it against you."

"But the damage is already done," she said glumly.

"That's not true." No, he couldn't believe that. "I'm sure if you talk to her, she'll understand."

"I—Oh God, Gabriel's coming back." Dutchy looked around in panic.

"I have fresh coffee for you," Gabriel announced as he stopped at their table, pot in one hand. "Let me tell you the specials," he began while filling two empty mugs. "Today we have rose lychee pie, burnt apple Camembert pie, and a Thai chicken *tom yam* pot pie that can be substituted for the beef pie with our lunch special."

The fuck? He had no idea what the hell came out from Russel's mouth, but it sure didn't sound like English. "I'll have the lunch special with beef pie and a slice of cherry with extra whipped cream for dessert."

"I'll have the same, please," Dutchy said.

"Coming right up."

As Gabriel was walking away, Dutchy called after him. "Gabriel?"

He whipped around. "Yeah?"

"Um, Gabriel ... is your fiancée around?"

"In the back." He jerked his thumb toward the kitchen door. "What's up?"

"Do you think I could ... if she's not busy back there, can I go in and talk to her?"

"Sure," he said. "Let me put your orders in, and I'll check with her, all right?"

"Thank you, Gabriel." She fiddled with her hair nervously and turned back to Krieger. "I'll apologize to her."

"Should be a good start." Though he had no idea what Gabriel's mate was like, she had to be very patient to put up with someone like Russel.

"Hey, Dutchy, I did you one better," Gabriel announced as he came back a minute later. He wasn't alone though, as a petite young woman with dark hair wearing an apron accompanied him. "This is my one and only mate, love of my life, Temperance Pettigrew. Temperance, this is Dutchy and Krieger."

"Hello," she said shyly. "Gabriel said you wanted to talk to me?"

"Yes I—Oh." Dutchy stared up at her, shock flashing across her face. "I-I-I ..." she stammered.

Krieger frowned, then realized what had caught her off guard. Temperance had a series of scars that started on her right cheek, going down her shoulder and arms. He'd seen some pretty bad burns in his career in the Special Forces, so he recognized them instantly.

Dutchy went completely red, her face crumpling. "I'm sorry!"

"No, no." Temperance sat down next to her. "It's fine. I'm used to it." Gabriel put a hand on her shoulder, and she looked up at him. Something passed silently between them, and it was as if they were the only people in the room. "It was a house fire, when I was a teenager," she continued when she turned back to Dutchy. "A long time ago, and I'm fine now."

He had no idea that Gabriel's mate was a burn survivor. It seemed an odd pairing, seeing as he'd always been dubbed "pretty boy," but it was obvious he was head over heels for his mate.

Dutchy straightened her shoulders. "I wanted to apologize to you, personally, for not getting back to you about your gown."

Temperance peered at her cast. "It's all right. J.D. and Anna Victoria told me ... told me that you've been working through some stuff."

"I really am sorry," she said. "I know timelines and things can be tight. When's the wedding?"

"In the spring," Temperance said. "Oh!" She clapped her hands together. "Is there enough time? Do you think you could still work on a gown? All these options from the wedding coordinator are terrible. I swear, sometimes it's like she works for Gabriel's sister and not us."

This time, Dutchy's face drained of blood. "I ... I ..."

Krieger discreetly cleared his throat and caught Gabriel's gaze. The lion shifter seemed to understand and squeezed his mate's shoulder. "Temperance, we can talk about it later, okay?"

"Of course." She stood up. "It was nice to meet you both. Enjoy your meal, and I'll see you around."

"I'll grab your orders, guys," Gabriel said and then led his mate away.

"Thank you," Dutchy said when they were far away enough. "For doing that."

"Doing what?"

"It's like ... like you know what I need. And you say and do the right things." Her lashes lowered. "So ... thanks."

He stared at her, stunned. She was easy to read, yes, but also, he was in tune to her every word and action so he could anticipate anything she needed. It was his job as her mate to take care of her. "You're welcome."

"This is making me think that maybe I need to start making amends." She fiddled with the coffee cup. "To go to my friends and apologize for ignoring them these past few months. I know they've all been worried about me. I mean, I've seen them at least once, because they've been helping me in the mornings, but I don't think I've ever told them I'm sorry. Maybe—"

"Here you go." Gabriel returned and placed three plates on their table. "Two beef pie specials. And a slice of rose lychee, compliments of the baker herself. Let me know when you want your dessert."

"Thank you," she said. "And please say thank you to Temperance too."

"Will do." Gabriel gave them a two-fingered salute as he dashed off to take another order.

The rest of the meal was spent eating in comfortable silence. Gabriel or Rosie stopped by to chat, refill their coffees, and serve them dessert. Krieger ate slowly, and whether consciously or not, soaked in every word and every movement she made. His mate really was gorgeous, even more than he remembered. Sure, she was looking a little thinner now, but that didn't detract from her beautiful face, smooth rosy skin, and all that vibrant red hair. His cock twitched just thinking about the times he had those red locks wrapped around his fist, her under him, being inside her.

He cleared his throat. "Scuse me." Before Dutchy could say anything, he stood up and strode to the men's room. *Calm down,* he told himself.

His bear, however, roared at him impatiently. It wanted now, more than ever, to claim her and make her theirs.

"Not yet," he said aloud as he stared at his reflection in the mirror. Dutchy wasn't ready. Her animal wasn't ready. Despite her congenial appearance, he could tell that her fox was still angry at him. But he didn't care; he was going to win her over. He'd wait forever if he had to.

After washing his hands, he went back to the booth. "Did you want anything else?"

"No, I'm pretty full." She winced and scratched at her cast. "Sorry. I'm just ... my shoulder gets tired easily. And *I* get tired easily."

"I'll take you home," he said.

After grabbing their check and paying, he led her to the truck, then drove her back to Angela's place.

"Wait," he began as she reached for the door handle.

"You don't have to walk me in," she said. "I can make it."

"It's not that." His mouth felt dry as a desert. "Dutchy ... will you have dinner with me? Tomorrow?" He already had it planned in his mind. Giorgio's, the Italian place on Main Street. She would have her dinner cooked by a professional chef and served by a waiter.

Her shoulders sank. "Krieger ... this was nice. It was good of you to take me out of the house and bring me to see Rosie. But, I'm not ready for a ... date."

The hope that had built up in him during the last two days suddenly deflated. "I see." His gut twisted, and he wanted to lash out. But his bear beat him—it clawed at him, urging him to not give up. Not on their mate. "I understand."

She gave him a curt nod. "Thank you."

He watched her hop out of the truck and scamper to the front door, frozen in place, chest aching like a giant fist wrapped around his torso. Why did it seem like instead of taking a step forward, he was actually jumping two back? Was all this work the last three weeks, giving her space and time, all for nothing?

Setting his jaw, he gripped the wheel tighter. No, he wasn't going to give up now. He would never give up on her. She was his mate; they were fated to be together.

His training in the Special Forces taught him to follow a plan through. But in the field, you had to be flexible to survive. So that's what he was going to do. Change tactics, but keep his eye on the prize.

Chapter 12

What the heck did I do to pass time these last months? Dutchy sighed for the hundredth time as she put her book down on her lap. She'd been reading the same paragraph for twenty minutes now. Not even the latest title from her favorite Regency romance author was enough to keep her attention.

I guess I'll have to wait and see if Nicola ends up with her duke. Tossing the book aside, she got up from the couch, stretched out her right arm, and walked into the kitchen to make herself some tea. Thank goodness she'd healed enough to take off the sling, but she still had to keep the cast on for another week or two.

After putting the kettle on, she sat at the table, staring at her empty mug. Her brain—and her fox—was telling her that turning Krieger down was the right decision. Did he really think he could just make everything better by sending her gifts and taking her on dates? It didn't work that way. How could she be sure he wouldn't just leave her again?

But her damn heart—and other sensitive parts of her, if she were honest—wanted to believe that he would stay. That this was it—the forever she'd been hoping for since her friends started pairing off.

"Dutchy!"

"What?" The sound of her aunt's voice and the piercing whistle of the kettle shook her out of her thoughts. "Oh. Sorry."

Angela had already turned the stove off. "Darling, are you okay? I walked in here, and you were just staring off into space."

"I ... I'm fine." Getting to her feet, she grabbed the kettle and poured hot water into her mug. "I was just woolgathering. You know. Do you want some tea? How was your day?"

"Oh, you know, the usual. Had two fittings and a new client." Angela blew at a lock of hair resting on her forehead. "Thanks, dear, but I think I'll need something stronger than tea after dealing with a total bridezilla."

"I've had my share of those," she said. "What happened?"

"She wanted this particular style that was on our social media page, but I already sold it out last week. When she found out, she blew her top and threatened to sue for false advertising. Then, she actually demanded I call the other bride and take the dress back and sell it to her—at a discount no less because now it was 'used.'" Shaking her head, she plopped down on the chair across from Dutchy. "Some people."

"Ugh, that sounds awful. I'm sorry."

"Like I said, I need something stronger tonight." Angela's eyes twinkled. "Say, how about you and I go out? Let's have dinner out and then maybe drinks? Where's that place all you young kids go to? That bar just outside town? The Pen?"

"You mean, The Den?"

"Yeah, that one. I'll probably be twenty years older than everyone there, but I'm sure they won't mind serving an oldie like me," she joked.

"Aunt Angela, you are *not* old," she admonished. Angela was over fifty, if she recalled correctly, but her hair was still vibrant and her skin smooth as someone ten years her junior. Like Dutchy, she was petite and curvy, and always dressed nicely, albeit more conservatively, preferring skirts that went below her knees and blouses that buttoned all the way up to her neck.

"I definitely feel old today." Angela eased her foot out of her heels and leaned back in her chair. "So, how about it, darling? Giorgio's and then The Den?"

She hesitated, but then gave it a second thought. Well, why not? She couldn't stay cooped up in here all the time. And when was the last time she spent time with her aunt? Growing up, she always admired and looked up to the sweet but pragmatic and sensible woman, who had an independent streak a mile wide. Of course, she never asked why Angela never married; her aunt was a private person when it came to personal matters.

"All right, Aunt Angela," she said. "Let's leave around six?"

Angela's face lit up. "Sounds fab!"

Later that evening as they split a bottle of wine and had some fabulous Italian food, Dutchy found herself having a good time. They had invited Rosie, too, but she asked for a rain check as she was busy closing up at the pie shop. After dessert and coffee, she and Angela drove out to The Den.

"Oh my." Angela glanced around as they entered the boisterous and noisy atmosphere of Blackstone's most popular hangout. Being a Saturday night, it was packed. "It certainly is ... something."

"I can go to the bar and get us more wine," Dutchy said. "And we don't have to stay long. If this isn't your scene, then we can always go back and open up that bottle of merlot in your cupboard."

"Dutchy! You're here!"

She turned her head toward the sound of the familiar voice. "Kate?"

Kate Caldwell-Thalassa enveloped her in a hug. "You made it."

Puzzled, she pulled away. "Made it?"

"She didn't put up a fight, did she?" Kate asked Angela.

Her aunt laughed. "Had to ply her with food and wine, but it wasn't hard."

"What are you guys talking about?" She placed her hands on her hips. "Did you plan this?"

"Nope." Kate shook her head, her jeweled nose piercing twinkling. "Not us."

"But who—"

"Come on." The she-wolf grabbed her hand and dragged her across the crowded room to a doorway leading to the back. "Hey, look who's here!" she shouted.

There were over a dozen people in the room, and they all turned toward them. Dutchy had to blink a few times because she realized she knew all these people. They were her friends.

"Dutch!" Amelia Grimes greeted as she dashed over. The tall bear shifter hugged her and then handed her a glass of white wine. "Glad to see you made it!"

"Me too," Penny Walker added. "Sorry I haven't come to see you or help out."

"It's fine, Penny." Penny had been her first client when she arrived in Blackstone. "I'm sure you've been busy running around after a toddler."

More people came up to her wishing her well, including her friends' respective mates, and to her surprise, the Blackstone Dragons themselves, Matthew and Jason Lennox, and their mates.

"Sybil sends her regards," Catherine Lennox said. She was mated to Matthew, the older of the twin dragons. "She really wanted to come and visit as soon as she heard about your accident, but she couldn't get away from her royal duties."

"She'll be here in a couple months, though," Christina said, her hand going to her stomach.

Dutchy's eyes widened as she saw the obvious bump of the other woman's belly. "Christina?"

Before she could answer, her mate, Jason, placed an arm around her. "Oh yeah. Finally knocked her up." The pride and joy on his face was brighter than the sun.

Christina rolled her eyes. "We've known for a while now and wanted to keep it quiet. But I just popped and couldn't hide it anymore."

"Congratulations, guys," she said. Despite the pang of envy in her chest, she really was happy for them.

"Our guest of honor is here!" J.D. exclaimed as she bounded over to them, Anna Victoria right behind her. "Glad to see you out and about, Dutch."

"Here, here," Anna Victoria added.

"Uh, thanks." She bit her lip. "But I'm still confused. Is this some kind of party? Someone's birthday?"

J.D. snickered. "Haven't you figured it out yet? This party is for you."

"For me?"

"Kinda," Anna Victoria added. "I mean, Krieger asked us to help track down anyone who might want to come and invite them here for a get together to cheer you up."

Blood rushed to her ears. "K-Krieger did this?" She glanced around at all the people gathered in the small room, chatting and laughing. Plus, there was a table on the corner piled with drinks and food, including pies from Rosie's.

"Of course." J.D. said matter-of-factly. "Who else would do this?"

"But where is he?" *And why hasn't he come up to me*, a small, disappointed voice in her added.

J.D. cocked her head toward the back of the room. Sure

enough, he was there, in the corner, chatting with Damon quietly.

God, how could one man look so good just standing there? He was wearing his jeans, leather jacket, and shirt combo again, though this time, he left his hair down.

Immediately, he must have sensed her gaze on him, because he looked up. Her heart leapt into her throat as their eyes met. He gave her a slight nod and took a slow sip of his beer.

J.D. nudged her with her shoulder. "So ... things going well there?"

"I—"

"Excuse me," a voice interrupted. "You're Dutchy, right?"

"Yes?"

The blonde woman who approached her was unfamiliar, but Dutchy knew at once she was a shifter.

"I'm Darcey. Darcey Wednesday," she introduced. "When J.D. told me where she was going tonight, I asked if I could come."

She held her hand out. "Nice to meet you, Darcey."

Darcey smiled weakly. "Um, I wanted to see if you're were okay." Her lower lip trembled as she peered down at her cast. "I-I was in the car that ran you over. It's a long story, but a group of bad men were trying to kidnap me."

"Oh." She recalled Anna Victoria telling her the story. "I'm glad they didn't hurt you."

"Yeah, they weren't able to get away ... but I'm *not* glad you were hurt in the process." Tears welled up in her eyes.

"Darcey, it's all right. Don't feel guilty. I'm here. I'm okay. They're going to take off the cast soon, and to be honest, it's more itchy than painful right now," she said, chuckling aloud.

Darcey brushed the tears away with the back of her hands. "I'm so happy to hear that. If it weren't for you and Krieger, I don't think I'd b-be h-here."

"Krieger?" For the second time that night, she was dumbfounded when hearing his name.

"Yeah, he was with Anders—that's my mate—when they came after me," Darcey explained. "He shifted and took down one of the guys who tried to kidnap me."

Krieger had been there? When she was struck down? Why did no one tell her that? Why didn't *he?* Darcey wrung her hands together. "If there's anything you need at all, please let me know."

"I—excuse me." A feeling from deep inside urged her to find him. Her fox hissed and protested, of course, but she ignored it.

She glanced over to where he was, now deep in conversation with Damon and another man who also wore the ranger uniform. Despite her stomach's churning, she made her way to him. "Um, Krieger?" Even now, she couldn't calm the pounding of her heart in her chest.

His gaze caught hers. "Dutchy."

"Can I talk to you? In private?"

The two other men looked at each other. "Why don't we go say hi to the boss, Anders? We'll chat more later, Krieg," Damon said, patting him on the shoulder. With a quick nod to Dutchy, he and the other man left.

"Everything okay?" Krieger asked, his tone concerned. "Are you tired? Does your arm hurt?"

"No, no. It's just ..." Her tongue tied up in knots, trying to find the words. "J.D. said you arranged this? Had all my friends come here to see me?"

"Yeah."

"But why? It's not my birthday or anything."

"I know. But the other night, you said you were a terrible person for ignoring your friends. I told you it's not true, so ... so I thought I'd show you."

"Show me?"

"That your friends care for you." The timbre of his voice lowered a notch. "Don't matter if you ignore them for months or years. Real friends pick things right up where you left them. And you don't have to ask them for forgiveness for things that weren't in your control. And if you do, they'll forgive you."

She stared at him, slack-jawed, unable to speak or do anything. *How does he do it?* How does he know the right thing to do or say? And why—despite her rejection yesterday—did he feel the need to do this for her?

The answer, of course, was there, but she couldn't verbalize it. Couldn't even think of it.

Straightening his shoulders, he finished the last of his beer. "Just stopped by to see you were okay. I should go—"

"No!" That came out more forceful that she meant it to. "I mean ... you don't have to."

His gaze slowly dropped to her hand. She did a double take, as she didn't even realize her arm had shot out and grabbed his forearm. Quickly, she withdrew it. "Will you stay?" Hesitation was evident on his face. "Please?"

"If you want me to."

"I want you to." She couldn't stop the corners of her mouth from quirking up. "You should at least enjoy the food and drinks. Have you had a chance to meet some of my friends?"

He shook his head. "J.D. and Anna Victoria did most of the work calling them up."

"Then you should come and meet them," she said. "C'mon."

They made the rounds of guests with Dutchy introducing him to everyone he didn't know. He was polite, though he only said one or two words at the most.

Kate and Amelia, of course, looked about ready to burst the entire time, but didn't say anything while Krieger was around. As soon as he excused himself to get her a drink, they practically cornered her.

Kate grabbed her by her good arm. "Is he—"

"Yes," she blurted out. "But you guys already knew that," she added wryly.

"Duh." The she-wolf rolled her eyes.

"I'm so happy for you," Amelia said. "I mean, I don't know the guy, and he looks a little scary, but if he's your mate, then I know he'll treat you right."

"He's hot too," Kate added in a low voice. "Sorry, you know my mate." She smiled and waved at Petros, who was carrying their daughter Sophia as he was chatting with Jason Lennox and Amelia's mate, Mason. "I swear, when I mention any guy is attractive, it's like a dog whistle only he can hear."

"Krieger *is* hot, though," Amelia added with a grin. "But not the type I thought you'd end up with."

"Who did you think she'd end up with? A certain silver dragon?" Kate waggled her eyebrows.

"Oh brother." Dutchy slapped herself on the forehead. "That again? The thing with Ian is ancient history. It's not like we're even friends now or anything."

"And nothing happened during the wedding reception at the palace?" Kate teased.

"Nothing." Her lips twisted. "Not that he didn't try."

Kate and Amelia cackled, and Dutchy found herself laughing with them. "Stop! I swear, you have one coffee date with a dragon and everyone thinks—oh, he's coming back." She cleared her throat. "Don't mention Ian, please? Or kilts."

"Kilts?" Kate asked. "What's wrong with kilts?"

"Hey, Krieger," Amelia greeted.

"Ladies," he grunted as he handed Dutchy a glass of white wine.

"Thanks, John," she said gratefully as she accepted the glass. "Oh! Luke and Georgina just arrived. I didn't realize you'd invited them too. Let's go say hello."

"We'll see you around," Kate said.

"Yes. More often now, I hope?" Amelia glanced meaningfully at Krieger.

Despite her initial hesitation, Dutchy enjoyed herself. She'd missed times like this—just hanging out with good friends, chatting and catching up. It was like things were normal again. Like she hadn't spent the last months pushing her friends and family away. No one seemed to hold a grudge against her, nor did they bring up anything about missed dinners, parties, or ignored calls and messages.

It was ... nice. And for once, that heaviness, that cloud that seemed to follow her around just disappeared.

As she mingled and caught up with her friends, she didn't notice that Krieger wasn't at her side. Not until Anna Victoria came up to her.

"This was a really great party," Anna Victoria said. "But Damon and I have to get going."

"So soon?" She glanced at her watch. "I've only been here two hours. Is it the baby? Are you tired?"

"Yes, and well, you know Damon," she said. "I'm surprised Krieger made it this long too."

"E-excuse me?"

Anna Victoria's brows furrowed. "You know. About ..." She nodded toward the exit, where Damon stood. The chief looked normal, but upon closer scrutiny, Dutchy did notice a few things. His rigid shoulders. The way he clenched and unclenched his jaw. The slight jitter of his right leg. And the thousand-yard stare that left his eyes vacant.

"You don't know," Anna Victoria concluded. "About them. The Special Forces. And Kargan."

"Kargan? What's a Kargan?"

Anna Victoria glanced around. "I'm sorry. It's not my place to tell you. And I don't know the details."

"Tell me what? Please," she implored. "I need to understand."

Anna Victoria paused, her eyes darting around. "Krieger and Damon were in the Special Forces together. Damon was his commander." She let out a breath. "There was an incident with an explosion in Kargan ... and then ... it's crowds for Damon, mostly. He doesn't like them because he was nearly trampled to death. Krieger, too, to some extent. He doesn't like being around others. Actually, I think this is the biggest crowd I've ever seen him in, except for the anniversary ball, and even then, he had to leave after thirty minutes when people started arriving."

What the heck was Anna Victoria saying? And why hadn't Krieger told her any of this?

"That's why he has to live all the way up there by Contessa Peak."

As if she wasn't reeling enough from processing this brand new information, the world halted under her feet at that last revelation. "Krieger ... lives there? In that cabin?"

"Yes. Damon visits him regularly. It's only recently he's been leaving on his own." Anna Victoria frowned. "Are you all right, Dutchy?"

She swallowed, trying to moisten her dry throat. All this time, she thought that cabin was just a temporary shelter. It had been his home. He had to live away from others. *I've been so blind.* So blind and focused on herself, she didn't see that Krieger had PTSD.

I've been working on it. Trying ... trying to be better. For you.

The realization crashed over her like a wave.

He lived alone, on top of a mountain because of some trauma that made it hard for him to be around others. He said he needed to stay up there. That's where he belonged.

But somehow, he was here. He made his way down from the mountain, fought with his demons and won.

Well, kinda.

Looking back on tonight, she realized how he got tenser with each interaction, his jaw hardening as the room filled up with more people, his stare becoming more vacant as the minutes ticked by. But he didn't say anything to her nor give any indication he wasn't having a good time. Hell, he even arranged this whole thing. *He was probably going crazy now with all these people here.*

"I need to go find him." Panic surged in her when a cursory glance around the room told her he wasn't there. "Where is he?"

"I don't know," Anna Victoria said. "Maybe he went to get some fresh air. That usually works with Damon."

"I'll try that. Thanks!" She made a mad dash for the exit, but didn't quite make it out as she bumped into someone also heading out.

"Dutchy!" Angela exclaimed as she grabbed her shoulders to stop them from falling over. "Dutchy, where are you going in such a rush?"

"I—sorry, Aunt Angela," she said apologetically. "I need to check on ... something outside. Are you all right?"

"Yes, darling, I'm fine," Angela assured her. "We're out of drinks, I'm afraid. I was wondering if Krieger knows where to get more? Should I talk to the bartender or manager?"

"Uh, ask for Tim at the bar, he should know." She gently pried Angela's fingers from her arms. "Sorry, but I really need to go now."

Crossing the crowded room, she made her way out the door. *Please be here*, she said to herself. *Please let me not be too late.*

The rush of air cooled her rapidly-heating cheeks. The lot was packed with cars, but devoid of any people. *Oh no.* Had the bar been too much for him? Was he gone? Did he have an episode?

"Dutchy? What are you doin' out here?"

Her skin prickled at the sound of the rough, low voice. Turning on her heel, she found Krieger leaning against the wall. His shoulders were hunched over, hands shoved into his pockets, moonlight illuminating his handsome face. However, looking past what was on the surface, she looked at him—really looked at him. The deep rise and fall of his chest as he struggled to breathe. The veins popping on his neck as he clenched his jaw. The racing of his heart that her shifter senses could pick up. It had cost him a lot to come here. But he did it anyway.

She took a step toward him. And another. Her fox hissed, as if to say, *don't you dare!*

Oh, shut up!

And she pushed it way down deep. *Stay there.*

"Dutch—" He flinched when her hands landed on his wrists. "Dutchy—your fox, it—"

"Doesn't matter." She searched his eyes. There was no spark now, and they remained a dull gray, but she still wanted answers. "Why didn't you tell me?"

"Tell you what?"

"That ... that place. The cabin. It was your home. You live up there, away from everyone. Why?"

A myriad of emotions passed across his face until it settled into a hard mask. "Doesn't matter."

"What happened, John?" Her hands slid up his arms and he flinched again. "Please. Tell me. What happened in the army?"

His jaw set. "I told you, it doesn't matter."

Freezing, she squeezed his bicep. "It's all right," she soothed. "You're not ready." Not now, anyway. He needed time to tell her.

Relaxing visibly, he said, "This isn't about me."

Everything I've done ... the last couple of months ... they've been for you.

These changes he'd been making ... coming down here. For her. To be with *her*.

"Dutchy? Are you—"

Something inside her propelled her forward, and she reached up to touch the sides of his face to pull him down and she pressed her mouth to his. He tensed, but only for a moment, then began to respond. His strong arms wrapped around her, lifting her up off the ground.

Oh. Her blood sang in her veins. His warm, firm lips caressed hers tentatively at first, but when she opened her mouth to urge him to deepen the kiss, he didn't need any more encouragement.

Suddenly, she found herself flipped around and pressed up against the wall, her knees lifted so she could wrap her legs around his waist. As his mouth descended down onto hers again, she melted against him, relishing the feeling of the muscles of his hard chest and being surrounded by his warmth and scent. He tasted like sunshine and earth and musk and everything she never knew she wanted until this moment. That's why she whimpered when he abruptly stopped.

"Are you hurt? Fuck, I wasn't thinking." He gently set her on her feet, then lifted her left hand up. "Your arm—"

"It's fine," she said. "I swear." *Damn cast!* Still, it was sweet that he thought of her comfort. "I'm fine."

He sighed with relief, then backed her up against the wall—carefully, this time—and cupped her jaw as he bent down to kiss her again.

She sighed at the soft exploration of his mouth. It was nice, but he seemed determined to handle her like some glass object. "Can I ask you for something," she said as she pulled away.

He leaned his forehead against hers. "Anything."

"Take me back."

His eyes flew open. "Back?"

"Up there. To the—your cabin."

"It's far," he said. "Nearly two hours to drive up."

"I don't care." She slipped her hands under his leather jacket, over his rock-hard abs and circled around his waist. Laying her head on his chest, she sighed. "Please."

The pleased rumble made her shiver. "All right." He pressed her tight against him, then kissed her forehead. "Truck's this way."

———

Krieger hadn't been kidding. It was a long drive up, which made her wonder to herself, *how did my fox make it all the way here?* She must have been really distracted to let her animal wander this far.

The vixen yapped at her, even as it was seemingly backed into a corner, ears flattened.

I said, shut it!

It whined and lowered its head.

Good. Her vixen was going to have to deal with being around Krieger, because this was happening.

Oh God, this was happening.

But then again, this was inevitable, wasn't it?

The truck slowed down as it rounded a corner, then drove off the path. They rumbled along, making several turns along the dirt road until a light appeared in the distance. As they got nearer, she recognized the cabin—his cabin, she corrected. Wiping the sweat from her palms on her jeans, she cleared her throat. "We're here."

He pulled up to the front of the cabin and cut the engine. "Yeah. Wait," he said when she reached for door handle. "The outside's slippery and not paved. Let me help you." He slipped out and rounded to her side, then opened the door. "Careful."

She smiled at him as he took her hand, then yelped in surprise as his other arm slipped around her waist to hoist her to his chest. "John, I can walk," she said with a half-protest, half-giggle.

"I know." He walked them over to the porch and set her down. "I just wanted to do it."

Heat spread up from her core at how their bodies touched. "Can we go inside now?"

Without delay, he opened the cabin then motioned for her to go in. "After you."

As she stepped inside, she took a deep breath. It smelled exactly as it did from her memories. Pine needles. Smoky wood. And Krieger. However, she did notice a few subtle changes. The dining table had two chairs now. There was also a well-worn leather chair in the corner next to a well-stocked bookshelf. She smiled to herself, wondering what kind of books he'd been reading.

"I—" Air rushed out of her lungs as he swooped her up and then deposited her on the bed in one motion. Ah, there was another change she noticed. "New mattress?" She bounced up and down to test it.

"Yeah," he said. "You said the old one was lumpy."

Had she? She didn't quite remember vocalizing it.

He slipped off his leather jacket and place it over the headboard. When he reached for the bottom of his shirt, he stopped. "Are you ... is this ..."

"Yes." She reached for the hem and inched it up, revealing his rock-hard abs and the mat of dark hair trailing down tantalizingly. His skin was hot where she touched him, her fingers moving up as she lifted the shirt higher. His pecs jumped when she pressed down on them, and the thumping of his heart against her palms brought a shiver of anticipation up her spine.

He yanked his shirt completely off and tossed it aside, then knelt on the bed next to her and fused their mouths together. Their lips barely left each other, not even when he slipped his shoes and socks off and pushed her to the center of the bed.

"Krieger ..." God, why was she nervous? It wasn't their first time. She knew his body well, and he knew hers. Yet, there was fluttering in her stomach she couldn't explain.

But there was no more time to be anxious as he grabbed the bottom of her sweater and pulled it off her, careful as he eased her left arm from the sleeve.

Oh, if only she knew how she would end up tonight, she would have dressed in something sexier than her white cotton bra and panties. However, from the desire etched on his face, it was obvious he didn't mind at all. He lowered his head, brushed her hair aside, and nuzzled at her neck.

"Beautiful," he murmured, licking and sucking at her skin. A sizzle of desire went straight to her clit, making it throb as her arousal intensified. His nostrils flared as he probably scented her wetness, and it only seemed to fuel his desire.

His hands were suddenly everywhere—cupping her breasts, unbuttoning her jeans and shucking them off, caressing her hip, digging his fingers into the soft flesh of her buttocks. Soon, she found herself on her back, knees spread.

"John!" She dug her fingers into his thick hair, pulling the scalp as his mouth devoured her through her cotton panties. Oh God ... it had been too long, yet she could never forget this. His lips and masterful tongue lapping, sucking at her with such enthusiasm that it should have been scandalous. He had pushed the fabric aside so he could lave her naked lips. It didn't take long before her hips were lifting off the mattress, and she came with the force of a gale wind.

"Dutchy," he growled low as he pulled her panties off. "I wanna be inside you so bad ... but I ..." A glance at her arm told her what he was worried about.

ALICIA MONTGOMERY

"Don't be worried," she cooed. Slowly, she sat up, then pushed him back down on the mattress. "Let's do it this way ... and we can take it from there."

His eyes devoured her, even as she could see the struggle in his expression. "You'll tell me ... if I'm hurting you."

"Of course," she assured him. Her fingers trembled when she reached for the fly of his jeans, but with minimal help from him, she managed to open them, exposing the dark furring of hair at his pubic mound. He lifted his hips to help her take off his jeans, and she couldn't take her eyes off the substantial tent of his briefs. Reaching inside, she took him out, gasping at the warmth and strength of his cock.

"Dutch—" He groaned and rolled his eyes back as she stroked him. He was like velvet and steel, and she reveled in the power she had over him, seeing how it drove him mad when she touched his cock. Leaning down, she pressed her mouth to the tip, and his hips rocketed off the mattress.

"Mmmm ..." She pushed his hips down, then enveloped the head of his cock with her mouth.

"Dutchy," he groaned as she took him in deeper, tongue licking and tasting him. The scent of him was overpowering, fueling her own arousal. She teased and sucked at him, letting him squirm and push his fingers through her hair to subtly direct her strokes. "God—Can't—"

She found herself pulled off him unceremoniously, then deposited onto his waiting cock. "Oh!" She was so wet, she slid down easily. He filled her to the root, and she could hardly move.

Krieger looked like he was barely hanging on, his fingers digging into her hips so hard they would surely leave a mark. So, she wiggled her hips, making him groan aloud. Placing her right hand on his chest, she leaned back, then slowly rocked back and forth.

From the way he threw his head back and his teeth bit into his lip, he was obviously enjoying himself, so she continued. Shifting her weight to her knees, she lifted her hips up and down, feeling him slide in and out of her.

"Fuck! That's good, baby," he said through gritted teeth as he reached up to caress her breasts. She rode him harder, faster, clenching around him as she watched his face twist with pleasure.

Pulling himself up, he shifted her again so they were face to face. His mouth captured hers, tongue delving into her like she was his first meal in a long time. She moved her hips harder, feeling her own pleasure building up.

"*Mmmph!*" She moaned into his mouth as he moved her again, this time, onto her back. Pushing her knees apart, he drove into her, rutting in hard and fast. She didn't even care about her cast, as she clung to him, hips meeting his every thrust. When he reached between them to pluck at her clit, she exploded, white-hot heat spreading through her body as she orgasmed. But he didn't stop, continuing to ride out her orgasm with her. Only when she was beginning to relax did he grunt and speed up, pushing—demanding for more—until she had no choice but to obey. When her body wracked with another orgasm, only then did he let go. His cock twitched inside her, filling her with his warm seed, his hips slowing to an erratic rhythm.

He kissed her again deeply as aftershocks rocked her body. Hands roamed over her breasts and sides, gentling as his fingers traced the pink, puckered scar on her torso. She sighed into his mouth as he withdrew from her, her body protesting at the loss.

How long they kissed and caressed and held each other, she wasn't sure. But her lips were swollen and her body boneless by the time he rolled off her and onto his side. An arm cradled her and pulled her to his chest.

She settled against him, fingers playing over the mat of hair over his pecs.

"Are you … okay?"

Her lips curled up at the corners at the question. "Better than okay." The satisfied rumbly growl from deep within his chest made her smile. She pressed a kiss to his side and turned her head up, planting her chin on him. "Thank you for taking me up here. And for the new mattress. I like the other changes, by the way." She noticed there was now a side table with a lamp and a clock.

His mouth actually quirked up. "I got new sheets and blankets too," he said. "Did I hurt you?" He glanced down at her cast.

"No, not at all." She hardly noticed it. It was probably the serotonin talking, though. "And before you ask … I'm not tired." Not even a little bit, she thought as her fingers moved lower, over his abs and continued following the trail of dark hair.

Heat filled his eyes. "Good. Neither am I."

Chapter 13

In his travels with the Special Forces, Krieger had seen some pretty marvelous sights. The sun setting over the Gobi Desert. Colorful birds while hiking through the lush forests of South America. The crystal-clear waters of the beaches of Zanzibar.

But for the life of him, he couldn't recall seeing anything as amazing as having his mate next to him on the bed, her brilliant coppery hair spilled over his pillows.

They'd made love for hours, until she was exhausted. Meanwhile, he hadn't slept at all, content to just watch the rise and fall of her shoulders as she breathed and the little movements of her eyes before she settled into a deeper slumber. He couldn't sleep, because he was afraid he would wake up alone and discover last night had all been a dream.

He didn't set up the party to seduce her into his bed again. Her rejection had stung, but it had all the more made him want to help her. All this time, he'd been trying to woo her and coax her with gifts and things she'd like, but it occurred to him that there was one thing from her old life that was still missing—the company of her friends. And so, he set up the party, even asking Angela to help get her to The Den.

He fought every instinct, every shadow, even his own bear, to be by her side as she introduced him to the people that mattered most to her. When it got too much, he had no choice but to rush outside. His bear didn't like the close quarters and needed to get out. It had been too crowded in there, too many people, too much noise.

It was the closest he'd been to losing control in the past couple of years. As much as he had changed on the inside, his grizzly was still feeling the scars, and having their mate so close without being able to claim her didn't help.

Yet here they were. She sought him out. Touched him, despite her fox's disapproval. And now that she was here, he would do anything to keep her in his arms and ensure they completed the mating bond.

A sound from the outside suddenly set his body on full alert. His bear got up on its hind legs, paws raised, ready to defend their den and mate.

Telling his animal to stand down—at least until they were able to investigate—he shifted Dutchy gently to her other side, careful that she didn't lie down on her arm. Slipping out of the bed, he quickly donned his discarded jeans and padded outside, readying himself for a fight if necessary. However, what he found at the bottom of his porch steps wasn't what he expected. Or rather, who.

The grizzled-looking wolf stared up at him with its one green eye, never breaking the gaze. Perhaps acknowledging Krieger's dominance and territory, the wolf lowered its head before it began to change. Matted gray and black fur receded into human skin, limbs shortened, and the figure stood up on two legs. "Hello, John Krieger," said the rough, accented voice of Milos Vasilakis. "It's nice to finally meet you."

Krieger stood up even straighter. "Milos," he greeted back. "To what do I owe this visit?"

Milos stretched his neck, popping and cracking the joints. His head was completely shaved and tattoos dotted his scalp, all the way down to his neck and chest. A patch of scar tissue covered where his left eye should be. "I was hoping to speak to you. About recent events in the mountains."

"Did you find the raccoon shifter?"

He shook his head. "There are other things I must speak to you about."

"What things?"

"Suspicions I have."

"You should talk to Damon about them."

"I know. But I wanted to run them by you. Damon may be your alpha, but he does not have your instinct. Nor does he know this territory as you do."

He huffed. "All right."

"May I come in?" he asked, cocking his head.

His instincts flared, knowing Dutchy was inside. His grizzly, too, did not like the idea of having another unmated male around her, especially since they hadn't bonded yet.

"Ah." His one green eye flickered over to his door, and Krieger shifted to block his view. "I see. You are not alone. Come," he cocked his head. "We walk and talk, yes?"

"All right." He hopped down the steps and followed Milos as he strode around the back. "So, what do you know about the missing raccoon?"

"I know of this shifter that Damon speaks of. A lonely creature, longing for something it lost." For a brief moment, a stricken look passed over the wolf shifter's face. "He comes regularly, every month or so, or at least he did until about two months ago."

"You know when he comes?"

143

"I know most of those who come up here regularly. Seeking solitude. Seeking peace. There are many who take advantage of the nature up here, to let their instincts take over and forget the human world for a little bit." Milos led them to a path around an outcrop of jagged rocks. "One is a sly little raven shifter who loves picking up shiny things that hikers may have lost or left behind. The little collector was especially active during the summer months. But it has stopped visiting."

"Maybe he's busy."

"Perhaps." As they rounded the boulders, they were treated to a view of the valley below and the splendid colors of the fall morning spread out beneath them. "But it was such a creature of habit and instincts. You must know how we cannot deny our instincts."

Krieger didn't miss the meaning in Milos's words or tones. But was he talking about him or himself? "Okay, so maybe another shifter is missing. What else ya got?"

"Strange scents in the air." Wolf shifters were known for their keen smell. "Like they do not belong up here, but they were manufactured to be."

"What the heck does that mean?"

Milos's lips tightened. "I cannot explain it. But I just know there is more to it than this. But nothing conclusive yet which is why I wanted to discuss this with you first. I know you have been ... preoccupied, but perhaps you could come with me on a patrol soon? That way, you can observe for yourself."

Krieger hesitated, but seeing as things had progressed with Dutchy—and protecting this territory was his job, in case he forgot—he knew what the right thing to do was. If Milos thought there was something fishy going on, then it was at least worth investigating. "All right. I have things to take care of, but I'll come out in a couple of days, if that works?"

"Thank you," Milos said, as they finished their walk around

the perimeter of the cabin and approached the front porch. "Perhaps Damon can—" The wolf shifter stopped short, mouth closing shut.

Krieger traced the other man's line of sight to the front door, where Dutchy stood, wearing only his uniform shirt. His bear reared up, and he rushed up to her, covering her from Milos's curious gaze. "You're up," he grumbled.

"I'm up," she repeated, then bent her head around him. "Hi there. I didn't realize there was anyone else up here. I'm Dutchy."

Every muscle in his body tensed, and although his every instinct screamed at him to push her inside, he controlled himself and his bear.

"I'm Milos," the wolf shifter greeted back.

Turning his head, he saw Milos had discreetly moved away, lest Dutchy saw his fully naked body. "Milos was just leaving."

"Leaving?" Dutchy asked.

To his credit, Milos nodded in agreement. "Yes. I shall see you soon, Krieger. And it was nice to meet you, Dutchy." Turning around, he shifted into his wolf and padded off into the trees.

"Who was that?" Dutchy asked.

"A ... neighbor." Now that the other male was gone, he could relax more. "Are you all right?"

Her arms slipped around him. "I am now," she breathed. "Didn't like waking up alone."

"Sorry." She would never wake up alone, ever, not if he could help it. "Are you hungry? Do you want some breakfast?"

Lifting her head up to him, she raised an auburn brow. "Let me guess—bacon, eggs, and toast."

He found himself grinning at her. "You bet."

"How about I make breakfast this time?" she asked. "And you can clean up."

"Whatever you want."

They headed inside, and Krieger put the conversation with Milos aside for now. Instead, he sat down and watched his mate as she puttered around the kitchen, humming to herself, dressed only in his uniform shirt. *This is how it should be.* How it should always be. And he would do anything to keep it this way.

"Can you light the stove and make coffee?" she asked swinging her head around.

Standing up, he sidled up behind her, brushing her backside with his hand and leaned down to nuzzle her neck. "Of course."

Breakfast didn't take long to cook as it wasn't anything fancy, though she did seem pleased at the addition of some spices and herbs to his cabinet. "They're from Damon," he said. "He usually brings me takeout or pizza when he comes by, and he got tired of trying to open those 'damn tiny pockets' of hot sauce and then spilling them all over his shirt."

They sat down, comfortable silence settling over them as they ate. "I didn't realize there were other rangers living up here," she began.

"Other rangers?"

"You called Milos your neighbor."

He bit into a strip of bacon, chewed, and swallowed. "He's not a ranger. Not really. Just a long-term guest."

"Ah."

There was hesitation in her eyes he couldn't miss. "Something wrong?"

"Nothing ... I mean ..." She pushed her eggs around her plate. "John ... will you tell me now what happened?"

"What happened?"

"Back ... back in the army." Pale, robin's-egg blue eyes peered up at him through thick lashes.

A cold sweat broke on his forehead as his muscles tightened. The fork he'd been holding bent in his grip. "We don't have to talk about that." Reaching for his cup, he took a sip of coffee, not caring if the liquid burned his mouth and throat.

"But, Krieger, I need to understand—"

"No!" He slammed the mug down so hard it broke and spilled coffee all over the table. Dutchy jumped and gasped. The fear there was unmistakable, and he immediately hated himself, but he couldn't control it. Rage boiled in him as he struggled to control his bear. It wanted out. It wanted blood. Pushing it deep down, he let out a roar and stormed out of the cabin.

He slammed the door behind him so hard, the walls shook. The cool air helped calm him, but it didn't ease the tightening of his chest or the pounding in his head.

I can't ... can't tell her. She could never know what *really* happened after Kargan. The nightmares that were still lurking ... it still seemed real.

The blood and destruction he left in the wake of his revenge spree sparked something in him and his bear. It wanted more. But there was no one left to hunt down. Everyone involved in the bombing had been removed from this earth, even down to the bomb maker who had pled for his life on his knees.

And so, he hid deep, deep in the Arak mountains in the darkest part of Kargan. He survived by hunting animals, sleeping in caves, or in dens he dug himself. But he hadn't been subtle about it. No, he left carcasses, went out at all hours of the day, sometimes ventured too close to farms.

His presence became some kind of legend throughout the villages in the mountains. Stories of the monstrous bear roaming the woods spread far and wide, becoming wilder and wilder with each telling. The beast was fifteen—no, twenty feet tall— with teeth like a saber-tooth tiger and claws tipped with poison. It roamed at night, stealing sheep—no, it could take horses or cows and swallow them whole without leaving any traces.

Then, when some child got lost and was found at the bottom of a ravine, they said it was the monster who did it, even though it was clear from the crushed bones that it was the fall that killed the boy.

The villagers wanted blood. A mayor offered a prize and promised the winner would be celebrated with a feast. They even made a stage where they would display the monster once it was caught.

So, they hunted him down. Sure, he was a powerful bear, but there were too many of them. And they had weapons and guns and nets. They set a trap for him. He had been desperate and hungry at the time, and he fell right into it. Cornered and fearing for his life, he had no choice. The only way to escape was to unleash his beast.

But his bear was still thirsting for blood, and so he took down several of them and killed two innocent farmers in the process.

Shock and guilt had made him shift back into his human form. They overpowered him. Imprisoned him. And not wanting to hurt any more innocent people, he didn't even put up a struggle as they hauled him off. Didn't fight them as they tortured him and left him half starved.

It was only by a stroke of luck that a passing truck with some British servicemen got lost and stumbled upon him, sitting in a cage in the middle of the village square. They contacted the embassy and the army, and that's how Damon had found him and brought him here.

He swallowed hard, as if he could consume the memories along with it and forget about them. Yes, he'd come so far. Made the changes. Got over the anxiety. Controlled his bear and bloodlust. Why couldn't that be enough for her? Why did she need to know?

She can't know.

She would forever see him as a murderer. Someone who shed innocent blood.

Unclenching his jaw, he spun around and entered the cabin. Dutchy was kneeling on the floor, mopping up the spilled coffee with a rag. She froze, then lifted her head. "I'm sorry," she said in a soft voice.

"No." He was at her side in two steps, and he gently lifted her to her feet. "*I'm* sorry. I was the one acting like an asshole. Forgive me?" *Please. Please say yes.*

"O-of course." But when he leaned down to kiss her, she put a hand up. "Just ... I know you've been working on yourself, these past months. It must have been tough. I can see that now. But I still need to understand. Promise me you'll talk to me about it?"

He said he would do anything to keep her. And so, he lied. "I promise."

Her shoulders relaxed. "Thank you."

A knife-like pain twisted in his gut at her sincerity. "Why don't you sit down and eat?" He grabbed the rag from her hand. "I'll take care of this, okay?"

"All right."

When he finished putting away the broken cup and the dirty rag, he sat back down.

"How long can we stay up here?" she asked, taking a bite of toast.

"As long as we want."

"No, seriously." She patted a hand over his. "Surely you have to work at some point. And I—oh no!" Worry marred her face.

"What's wrong?"

"Aunt Angela. We just left without telling her or anyone where we were going. She must be worried. I should call her."

She tried to get up, but he stopped her by placing a hand on her arm. "John—"

"Don't worry," he assured her, then pulled her to his lap. "I'm sure she can guess by now where you are. Besides, there's no phone reception up here. I can radio down to Damon and ask him to call her, if you want."

"I ... maybe." She looked so cute chewing at her lip, he had to kiss her. "But John, don't you have to work? Is that why Milos was here?"

"Kinda. I'm taking some time off now," he assured her. "I'm not going AWOL or anything. Damon said I can take as much time as I need. But ... I'm not keeping you locked up here with me. Not when you have your life and your friends back in town. We can go back now if you want."

She glanced around. "Being trapped up here with a sexy man with nothing but a bed? Doesn't sound like a bad deal to me." Her hips shifted, and her core rubbed against him, making him groan. "But ... you're right, I do need to go back down at some point, and you're much better now, right? You don't have to stay up here all the time. So ... how about another day? Let's spend the day here and then we can go back to town tomorrow."

"Sounds good." He nuzzled at her throat, then stood up without letting go. "Now that we're done with breakfast, how about some dessert?"

———

Heading back to town the next day took much longer than Krieger thought. It wasn't so much the drive itself, but rather, it was getting started. Neither of them was in a hurry, and despite spending most of the previous day inside, they had yet to tire of each other's company.

They agreed on leaving after breakfast, but ended up

spending most of the morning in bed again, so then he cooked them some steaks for lunch. Afterwards, they took a walk around the woods. By the time they got back, it was late afternoon.

It wasn't like they had a timetable. No, Krieger didn't dread coming down from his cabin, not with Dutchy now at his side. But there was a small kernel of doubt growing in his mind.

She said she forgave him after his outburst yesterday. He believed her words, but couldn't help but feel that there was still a gap between them, an invisible divider that still kept her truly out of his reach. Plus, it bothered him that he couldn't reach her fox.

It was disappointing, because he wanted to see the pretty little thing again, but it loathed him, hissing and barking when he tried to reach out. And frankly, it irked him that though he had won over Dutchy, her animal was still being stubborn. His bear, too, did not like it and roared at him to make things right with the vixen.

You're the shifter, he grumbled to his grizzly. *Why don't you fix things with the fox?*

The damned bear just sat back on its fat ass, arms crossing over its chest.

Dutchy had fallen asleep halfway through the drive, but as he made the turn off from the mountain road, she stirred. "Where—oh." A yawn escaped her mouth, and she stretched her arms over her head. "Sorry. Must have drifted off."

"Didn't want to wake you. You seemed exhausted."

"Didn't sleep much. Not that I mind." She smiled saucily at him.

"We'll be at Angela's soon," he said.

"Oh. Right." Sitting up straight, she cleared her throat. "So, the cast is coming off my arm next week, though it doesn't really bother me much anymore." She gave a nervous laugh. "So, I was thinking of moving back into my place."

"You are?" He didn't like the idea of her being alone and vulnerable in that house by herself. Plus, he remembered the state it was in. *Should have cleaned up.* But he didn't do anything more than repair the lock when he came back the next day.

"Yeah. Aunt Angela's been so nice and patient, taking care of me, but ..."

"She's your family, of course she wants to do that for you."

"I'm not being ungrateful. But I can't live there forever. And I'm sure she'd like her home and privacy back." She fiddled with a lock of her hair. "And so will ... we."

It took him a second to get her meaning. "Oh."

"Yeah. Angela's always been sweet and kind, but also prim and proper. Not that she's a prude, but she probably won't like the idea of having a strange man under her roof. I mean not that you're strange." She slapped her hand over her mouth.

"No explanation needed," he said quickly. "And it's true. I'm practically a stranger to her."

"And with her being a shifter, I don't think she'll want to listen to us all night long." Her cheeks pinked adorably. "Besides, we're not both going to fit into the double bed in her second bedroom."

"You ... you want me to stay? With you?"

"Of course. When you're down here," she added. "I won't be ready to move out right this minute. Oh God." Her fingers massaged her temples. "My house! It's probably in a terrible state. I haven't even thought of the trash I left in the kitchen or my dishes in the sink. It might be a day or two before we can be together again. But at least you won't have to make that long drive every day."

"Don't mind at all," he said. "I'll drive home tonight or crash at Damon's." If Angela wasn't comfortable with him in her home, then he would understand. "We can start cleaning up your place tomorrow." Before she could protest, he announced, "We're here."

He pulled in front of the ranch-style home, then cut the engine. "Hold on," he said, and got out of his side to circle around to help her out.

"You don't have to keep doing that," she said as he opened the door.

"I want to," he said. Any chance to touch her, he would take, especially if he might not be in her bed tonight. He and Dutchy were adults, of course, but maybe she didn't want her maiden aunt's disapproving eye—or ears—on them.

"Hmm ..." She kissed him, then tucked her hand into his arm as they strode up the walkway. Keys in hand, she slipped them into the door and pushed it open. "We should—" She froze and stopped halfway as voices streamed into the front hall. There was a shriek, followed by a low grunt.

"Aunt Angela!" Dutchy grew pale.

Krieger's bear reared up, ready for any danger. "Stay here!" Pushing Dutchy behind him, he dashed to the kitchen where the sounds were coming from, claws out and ready to pounce. As he burst through the entryway, he stopped short, his brain short-circuited for a moment as it tried to process what he was seeing.

Angela was planted on the counter, head thrown back as a large, hulking man stood between her knees, pants down to his ankles, furiously pumping away as the female shrieked in what sounded like ecstasy and delight.

"Krieger!" Dutchy ran, stopping right behind him. "Is she okay—holy moly!"

Dutchy's exclamation caught the lovers' attention, and Angela's vocalizations halted as her gaze dropped to them. "D-

Dutchy! Y-You're home." Needless to say, her face turned redder than a tomato.

"Aunt Angela, what the—" Dutchy gasped when the man between her aunt's legs turned his head, revealing none other than The Den's owner himself. "Tim?"

Though he'd only met the polar bear shifter a few times, Krieger would have described him as stoic and unflappable. At this moment, however, the look of pure surprise on his face was incredibly comical. "Aww, *fuck*," he cursed as he bent down to pull his pants up. "Uh ... this ain't ... I'm not ..." Securing his belt, he turned to face them. "Didn't think you'd be back so soon."

Angela gulped a lungful of air as she pushed her skirt down, then slipped off the counter. "Uh, how was your day, darling?"

Dutchy buried her face in her palms. "I need a moment here." Turning on her heel, she walked out the door.

Krieger shifted uncomfortably. "So ..." None of them could meet each other's eyes. "I'll ... go check on Dutchy."

He walked out of the kitchen and into the living room. Dutchy was pacing across the carpet, mumbling to herself. "You okay?"

"Oh God, I'm going to be scarred for life."

He frowned, trying to figure out what would be appropriate to say at this moment.

"I mean," she stopped and then scratched at her head. "Angela's an adult, free to do what she wants. It's just kinda ... surprising. He's not at all the type of guy that I pictured with her. Not that I think he's not good enough. Though she's my aunt and the sweetest person in the world, and no one's good enough for her. However, I'm pretty sure they'd only ever met the night of the party, and that was the day before yesterday, and now they're doing the nasty on the kitchen counter." She continued her pacing.

He opened his mouth, but she cut him off.

"Good for her, though. I'm not shaming her for having some fun, if that's what she wants. But he better not hurt her or take advantage of her. Of course, we all know Tim, and he'd cut his own hand before he hurt any woman, so there's that." Striding over to him, she patted him on the shoulder. "Thanks so much."

"Thanks? For what?"

"For working that out with me. You've been a great help."

God, she was so adorable and beautiful like this. Of course, he couldn't blame her if she was having a mini stroke; *he* was going to be scarred for life, too, and he would never unsee the sight of Tim Grimes's hairy ass thrusting away like a piston. He'd never be able to walk into The Den again and meet him in the eye. *Might have to tell Damon to find another place to hang out.*

"Dutchy?" Angela entered the living room, clothes and hair in place, her hands wringing together. "I-I'm sorry you had to see that." Her complexion had yet to return to its normal color. "We, uh, weren't expecting you."

I bet, Krieger thought to himself. "We didn't tell you when we left the other night," he said instead. "Apologies, ma'am, if we caused you any worries."

Angela smiled warmly at him. "I knew she was in safe hands."

"And so were you, it seems like," Dutchy guffawed, giving her aunt a hip bump and eyebrow waggle. "So ... you and Tim, huh?"

If it were possible, she blushed deeper. "We uh, got to know each other the night of your party when I came up and asked him about the drinks. Well, actually, he seemed kind of grumpy because he was busy, but I just didn't know what to do. Then he helped me and brought in more drinks, and we got to talking ... well, stuff happened. I know he's probably not the most conventional choice for me, but ... I like him. And we've decided to keep seeing each other exclusively and see where this goes."

"That's great, Aunt Angela. If you like him and he likes you, then I'm all for it." She drew her in for a hug. "Just ... leave a sock on the door next time, huh?"

The sound of throat clearing caught their attention, and Tim's tall figure filled the doorway. "Hello ... uh ... awfully sorry, Dutchy," he began, his bushy white brows drawn together. "Meant no disrespect to you or your aunt. She's a special lady, and I plan to treat her as such."

"It's fine, Tim," Dutchy said. "We're all adults here. And we really should have called ahead."

Tim's arm came around Angela and her face lit up like a Christmas tree. "Well, I was going to make some dinner ... maybe you can help me, Dutchy?"

"Oh no. Nuh-uh." She shook her head. "I love you, Aunt Angela, but it'll be a while before I can step into that kitchen again."

Unable to stop himself, Krieger barked out a laugh, then coughed to cover it when Tim glared at him. "Scuse me," he said "Dusty in here."

"I'll take care of dinner," Tim said, kissing her on the forehead. "Was gonna do the steaks out on the grill anyway. Want to help me, son?" he asked Krieger.

"Sure, Tim."

"You ladies put your feet up." Tim nodded to the couch. "That bottle of red should have had time to breath. Pour yourselves a glass while we get the food ready."

Maybe it was the atmosphere or the five beers he had while helping with dinner, but Krieger found himself relaxing, though it was still hard to meet Tim's gaze without wanting to crack up or look away. He wasn't much of a cook, so all he did was chop up the salad and mashed the potatoes while the polar bear shifter worked on the grill out in the backyard.

"Need to ask you something," Tim said as he came into the kitchen, platters of steaks in hand.

"Uh, sorry. Don't have word on your friend yet."

The polar bear shifter's lips thinned. "Didn't think so. But that wasn't my question." He glanced at the doorway to the living room as Angela and Dutchy's mingled voices and laughs drifted in. "You make things right with her yet?"

He frowned. "Working on it. But headed the right way."

"Good. Angie's been worried about her. And I can't have her bein' unhappy."

"Aren't you going a little too fast?" Krieger shot back. "You only met her two days ago."

"Fast?" Tim placed the platter on the kitchen counter and faced him. "I've been on this earth for nearly six decades, sonny. What more have I got to wait for?"

"How about your mate?"

"Not sure if I have one. You know that's not a guarantee."

True. His parents and grandparents weren't mates and they were perfectly happy. In fact, Grandma and Grandpa Krieger were about to celebrate their sixty-third wedding anniversary next year.

"But I know a good woman when I see one," Tim continued. "And I ain't wasting no more time waiting for something might not be in the cards for me. When you find something you want and that's worth it, you hang on to it for dear life. Fight for it if you have to."

Now that he could agree with. "Amen."

"Everything okay in here?" Angela asked as she poked her head in. "That smells delicious by the way."

"We're all good, Ange," Tim assured her. "If you wanna set the table, we can eat in five."

"Great!"

Soon, they were all sitting down at the dining table, enjoying their food and drinks. This wasn't how he had thought the night would end. No, it was better, especially when he saw how happy and carefree his mate was.

"Thank you for the dinner, it was delicious, Tim," Dutchy said. "By the way, Aunt Angela, I wanted to let you know I'll be moving back to my place as soon as I can get it cleaned up."

"I anticipated that, darling," Angela said. "You haven't needed anyone's help around the house in a while. That's why I had a cleaning company come to your house today."

"Y-you did?" Dutchy's auburn brows furrowed together.

"Just your kitchen, bathroom, and bedroom, darling," Angie clarified. "And Tim and I were there supervising the entire time.

"Oh. Right." She swallowed. "Thanks, Aunt Angela, that's really nice of you. My place was probably in a terrible state."

"Noticed your car'd been sitting in the garage for too long, there was a leak underneath. Tires needed rotating too," Tim added. "Took it to J.D. myself to get checked out. She says she'll bring it by tomorrow."

"That's really nice of you, Tim," Dutchy said. "Thank you both."

"No worries, darling. Now," she stood up. "I'll get coffee and dessert."

Krieger couldn't help but notice that there was still tension on Dutchy's face. Leaning over, he asked, "Are you okay?"

"I'm fine," she said, smiling up at him, though it didn't quite reach her eyes. "Really. Just ... stuffed from this meal."

Angela came back with a tray that had a carafe of coffee, plates, and a small cheesecake. "Here you go." As she sat down to cut and distribute the cake and cups, she nodded to Dutchy.

"Darling, could you grab the sugar behind you on the counter? Thanks."

Dutchy reach behind her and placed a small red canister on the table next to him. Grabbing the container, he put a healthy teaspoon into his coffee, stirred it, and took a sip. A second later, the unexpected taste of salt coated his tongue, and he spit out the hot liquid.

"John!" Dutchy exclaimed as she handed him her napkin. "Are you all right?"

"I ... yeah ..." he sputtered as he wiped his beard. Good thing he didn't spray it out, and it only dribbled over Angela's white linen tablecloth. "Sorry."

"What's the matter?" Angela asked, concern marring her face. "Was it too hot?"

He shook his head and took a big gulp of water from his glass.

Angela frowned. "I—oh!" She cocked her head at the red canister. "Darling, that's the salt. Sugar is blue, remember?"

Blood drained from Dutchy's face. "I ... sorry, I must have grabbed the wrong one. S-sorry, John."

His heart clenched at the pain on her face. "It's all right, Dutchy," he said in a quiet voice. "It was an honest mistake." But from the way her hands shook and her lower lip trembled, he knew it wasn't that simple and he remembered why.

Dutchy could still not see any color.

Had he forgotten that part? That his initial rejection of her had fundamentally broken her so much that it not only made her animal hate him, but also reduced her ability to create her art?

But why had her sight not returned to normal yet? He'd done everything he could to make her better.

Obviously not everything. The mating bond hadn't formed

yet. Her fox still could not stand him. What else hadn't he done for her?

Thankfully, Angela's sweet and caring nature soothed his mate, and Dutchy seemed more at ease as the evening wore on, and they continued to chat over coffee and dessert, lingering until it was nearly midnight.

"I think we should get going," Dutchy declared with a yawn. "Can I stop by tomorrow to pick up the rest of my stuff? I promise I'll call first," she added with a grin.

"Of course, darling," Angela said with a chuckle. "You can come anytime."

Tim cleared his throat.

"How about later? Noonish?" Angela added with a wink to Tim.

"That's fine, Aunt Angela."

They got up, helped put the dishes away in the kitchen, then said their final goodbyes and left. As they drove, Dutchy seemed distracted enough that she didn't question how he knew where her house was located.

When they walked into her home and the silence of the place settled over them, he put a tentative hand on her shoulder. "Do you need to ... talk?"

She shook her head. "I'm just tired, okay?"

Not wanting to press her, he nodded and kissed her on the forehead. "Why don't you get ready for bed? I'll be right behind you."

She made a non-committal hum and padded down the hallway to the bedroom. As her aunt promised, the entire place was sparkling clean and smelled of lemon, carpet cleaner, and wood polish. He wished he'd thought to do some cleaning when he came here to find out more about Dutchy, but—

Wait.

His head swung to the door on the other end of the living

room. Her office. And he recalled now Dutchy had been alarmed that the cleaning crew had come in. And how relieved she'd been when Angela mentioned they only worked on the other rooms.

She didn't want them to see. Didn't want Angela to see what was in there.

I'm an idiot.

He said he was going to fix her, but the job was far from done. How could it be, when that one thing about her, the part that was most important to her—her talent and creativity—was still broken?

Well, he'd come this far, so he wasn't going to stop now. He just needed to push her in the right direction again. And he had an idea just how to do that.

Chapter 14

Dutchy couldn't believe this was her house. She peeked into the kitchen and saw all the trash and takeout containers were gone and the dishes put away. It even smelled clean in here. *Thank you, Aunt Angela.* But then, it was just like her to do something like this.

While she'd been hesitant at her aunt's blooming romance with Tim Grimes—and mildly horrified considering how she found out—Angela had assured her she was happy. "I know you think it's going fast, darling, but at my age, you can't waste any more time," she had said with a laugh. "And sometimes, when you know, you just know." Her words, plus the obvious adoration in the polar bear shifter's eyes when he looked at her aunt, made Dutchy feel relieved. It was going to be interesting to see this play out.

Indeed, it had been a wonderful evening. At least it was. Until she was reminded again of her current situation.

She clutched at the twinge in her chest. It wasn't like she could forget about her visual impairment. But these past few months, she had gotten used to it. And when she was with Krieger, she could almost forget it was an issue. He made her feel like everything was right and perfect. Sure, her vixen still acted pissy around him, but for the most part, it stayed quiet and didn't hurt her anymore. Maybe things would get better from now on, and her fox just needed time.

Heading into the bedroom, she walked over to her closet. All her clothes had been washed and folded neatly inside. Grabbing a pair of pajamas, she headed into the bathroom. *Hot shower, finally.*

Heavy footsteps from behind made her pause. Her fox, as always, chuffed distastefully at Krieger's presence, but she ignored it, as she did the crushing disappointment at her ineptitude. Turning her head, she grinned at him. "I'll need some help soaping up. Wanna join me?"

The heat in his eyes was unmistakable, and from then on and for the rest of the night, they didn't talk about what happened during dinner.

The next morning, she woke up alone in bed. *Huh.* The trace scents on the pillow and sheets told her Krieger hadn't been gone long, though. There were no sounds in the bathroom, so where could he be?

Hauling herself out of bed, she put her robe on and padded out to the kitchen. The coffee maker was full, but no sign of Krieger. Did he get breakfast? He wasn't in the living room either, and his truck was still outside. Where—

Her enhanced hearing picked up some shuffling sounds. And when she realized where they came from, she paused.

Spinning around, she headed for her office. Despite the bile churning in her stomach, she made herself go in there. Sure enough, Krieger was in there, pinning up her sketches to the wall. The outfits she had ripped off the dress forms had been placed back on them, and seeing them made blood drain from her face. "W-what are you doing?"

He swung his head toward her, his expression turning

sheepish. "Didn't think you'd wake up so early. Wanted to surprise you."

Her fingers curled into her palms. Despite her throat closing up, she managed to speak. "S-s-surprise?"

"Yeah." He finished pinning up the drawing behind the second dress form. "Angela didn't get to clean up in here and—"

"How dare you!" Anger rose in her as her fox hissed and snarled at him. "This is a total invasion of my privacy." Pain stabbed at her being in this room for the first time in months. And her dresses and the sketches she never wanted to see again were now displayed, mocking her with their mere presence.

"Dutchy?" He gaped at her. "What's the matter?"

"What's the matter?" She stomped into the room, rage and hurt fueling her. "I didn't tell you to do ... this!" Glancing around, she saw her drafting table had been cleaned up as well, her brushes and pens back in their holders. Her knees weakened as she strode over and saw that the half-finished sketches and scrawls she had crumpled and tossed had been carefully smoothened out. There it was, her failure out in the open on display. Like a bleeding wound.

"Dutchy?" Krieger rushed to her side. "Dutchy, please—" He tried to touch her, but her fox lashed out. "What did I do?"

"What did you do?" Her eyes narrowed at him. "Are you mocking me? Showing me what a failure I am?"

"Jesus, Dutchy, no!" He scrubbed his palm down his face. "No, no! I'm not. I only wanted to show you how proud I am of you. Of how talented you are—"

"*Were*," she corrected.

"Stop it," he said. "You *are* talented. And I came here to show you. To—"

"Fix me?" she finished. "Is that what this is about? I'm like some broken toy you want to fix?"

"No, I—"

165

"I'm never going to design again. Can't you see that? *Never*."

His jaw hardened. "Yes, you will. And if you don't, then it doesn't make you any less of a person. I'll take care of you, I promise."

That should have comforted her, but it didn't. Being in here was a painful reminder of what she once was. And how lacking she was now and how her fox continued to hate him. "You don't know that." As he came closer, her vixen opened its mouth and let out an angry bark. "And how can you possibly fix me when you can't fix yourself?"

That comment hit its mark, and the look of hurt on his face couldn't have been more evident. But it was like she was riding a rollercoaster, and she had reached the top and couldn't back down now. Her fox, too, goaded her on. "When are you going to tell me what happened to you back in Kargan?" Had she forgotten about yesterday's incident? Her fox sure didn't. It reminded her about how he had lost control when she asked him during breakfast. "I didn't even know that you were in the army and Damon was your commander. I had to find out from Anna Victoria. Do you know how humiliating that was?"

"It doesn't matter. None of that matters."

"None of it matters?" she echoed, her voice rising. "Stop patronizing me and treating me like a child. Are you going to keep things locked up from me and then lash out when I say or do something wrong? Were you even planning on telling me?" His silence said it all. "So, you lied to me when you said we would talk about it! Did you even think—"

"I said it doesn't matter!" he roared. "Just forget it. I'm past all that. I've already changed for you, is that not good enough? Am I not enough now? All I wanted was to be left alone up there, then you come along, and now I'm doing all these things for you."

"I didn't ask you to change!" she shot back. "No one asked you to do these things!"

He charged toward her desk, swiping the Vogue magazine off the top. "Is *he* what you want? Someone who's handsome and rich and whole? Why don't you go back to him then?"

Her rage boiled over. "Fuck you, John, this is not about Ian, and you know it!" Tears welled up in her eyes, but she refused to let him see it. Whirling around, she hugged her arms around her stomach. "You ... you should go." She closed her eyes, the tears already tracking down her cheeks. Heavy footsteps thudded out of the office and thundered toward the front hall. The slamming of the door made her jump, and she sobbed into the back of her hand, then sank against the wall.

The tears wouldn't stop, and she continued to weep, her chest collapsing in on itself and the pain making it hard to breathe. *How did they end up like this?* Maybe it was inevitable. The rush of desire and the headiness of the sex was like a fog covering up all the underlying issues still between them. He refused to open up about his past. And she was still so afraid that he was going to hurt her.

Yet his words echoed in her mind even now.

It doesn't make you any less of a person. I'll take care of you, I promise.

Wiping her tears away, she glanced around the room. He must have woken before her to clean up in here. There was no layer of dust on the surfaces, and the hardwood floor had been swept and polished. All her pens and brushes were back in their holders. He even carefully taped up her torn drawings and put her dresses back on the forms.

It was obvious now he had meant no malice in his actions, just like all the other nice things he did for her, like taking her to Rosie's and organizing the party with her friends. His intention really was to show her how proud he was of her work. And that he believed her normal vision would return. "Oh God." She shouldn't have flown off the handle. *I made a mistake.*

She rushed out of the office and scurried out the front door, her stomach dropping when only the empty driveway greeted her.

Regret filled her as she remembered her actions and words. *I should have been more understanding about his situation.* The scars he carried were much deeper than she thought. "I promise, John, we'll get through this together."

Heading back inside, she plopped down on the couch. Where could he have gone to? *How am I going to contact him?* He didn't own a phone. Would Damon know how to reach him?

The sound of an engine pulling up outside made hope soar in her chest. *He's back!* She'd tell him how sorry she was for jumping to the wrong conclusions and kiss him and never let go.

She practically flew to the front door and yanked it open. "John!" She threw her arms out. "I'm so—J.D.?"

"Whoa!" The blonde mechanic started, but stepped forward and hugged Dutchy back anyway. "I'm glad to see you too!" she said with a laugh.

"W-what are you doing here?"

"Came by to drop off your car." She jerked her thumb back at the familiar Honda in the driveway and dangled her keys in front of her.

"I—oh!" Krieger was probably on his way back to his cabin. She could go after him and apologize. "Thanks for getting that all done. Send me the bill, I'll take care of it."

"Nah, on the house. But, say, how did Tim manage to get your keys?"

"Er, long story." She grabbed her keys from J.D.'s fingers. "I need to go." Sidestepping around J.D., she zipped toward her car.

"Go? Hey, wait!" J.D. chased her. "Go where? Can you even drive?"

She glanced down at her arm. *Ugh, stupid cast.* It didn't hurt, but it probably wasn't safe to be driving up those mountain roads without the use of both her arms. "Dammit!" Tears sprang into her eyes again.

"Did you—hey! Dutchy?" J.D. touched her arm. "Dutchy, what's the matter?"

"Oh, J.D.," she sobbed. "I've ruined everything." And so she told her friend about what had transpired that morning with Krieger. "I'm an asshole, J.D. I shouldn't have said those things and then kicked him out. He's got PTSD, and I should have known better."

J.D. blew out a breath. "Hey, c'mon now." Fishing out a handkerchief from her pocket, she handed it to Dutchy. "Krieger's had a hell of a time, and I can't even begin to imagine what could have happened to him. But I know Damon was in bad shape when he came back, and I had to kick him in the butt a few times to snap him out of it. Even now after he's met Anna Victoria, he's still working on his own shit. And remember, you haven't exactly been in the best place yourself. Cut yourself some slack."

"I just ..." She blew her nose. "I'm afraid I've ruined everything, now."

"What? Are you kidding me? You guys had a little tiff, that's all." She enveloped Dutchy in another tight hug and then looked her square in the eyes. "Krieger obviously adores you. He'll forgive you for anything. If it'll make you feel better, I'll drive you up there."

"Y-you will? What about work? Your garage?"

"I'm the boss." She rolled her eyes. "If I haven't trained those jackasses how to get stuff done without me by now, then I don't deserve to be in charge. Besides, they'll be happy I'm not there to ride their asses today."

"I ... thank you, J.D."

"Cheer up, buttercup," J.D. said, beaming at her. "C'mon. Get dressed. We'll stop for coffee and gas, then head up. It's gonna be a long drive. Maybe you can tell me that story about Tim and your car."

Chapter 15

K rieger drove back up to his cabin in what seemed like record time. The truck careened through the mountain roads, hugging the sharp curves. He really didn't give a shit if he was going too fast. If he were a lesser man, he would have driven right off.

How the fuck had things turned tits up in five minutes? He'd gotten up early, fixed up her office to surprise her, and then she goes all crazy. *Women.* Who the hell knew what went on in their brains?

As he drove up the dirt road, the engine roared, and the truck's tires skidded. *Must have rained hard.* He shifted the truck to all-wheel drive and then continued on until he reached his cabin. He stormed inside and shut the door with a thundering bang. Of course, the first thing that hit his nose in here was the scent of Dutchy and sex.

"Fuck!"

Turning on his heel, he headed out the door and sat on the porch steps, burying his face in his hands.

Her outrage at his invasion into her personal space he could handle. He read her wrong. But why did she go and turn it all around and ask about Kargan? Couldn't she leave well enough alone? It was all in the past. He was over it. She didn't need to know. He couldn't let her know. The ache in his chest grew like a fucking tumor, squeezing around his lungs until he couldn't breathe.

His bear roared in pain. It, too, felt her anger and rejection. Because that's what this was, right? Her fox still refused him. And the mating bond would never happen if the vixen didn't accept him. He didn't know why he knew that; he just did.

"Krieger?"

His head snapped up so fast the blood rushing to his head made him dizzy. "Chief?" He'd been so caught up in his head that he didn't even hear Damon approach him. His former commander wore only a pair of jeans, his shirt in one hand, which meant he'd come up here in bear form. "What are you doing here?"

He slipped his shirt on. "My bear hasn't been in the best mood. Since the news about the cub ... it ... I mean, *we've* been feeling over protective, and Anna Victoria got sick of the whole thing. Said I was smothering her," he said sheepishly. "So, she's having dinner out with Sarah and Darcey tonight after they close up, and I thought I'd let my damned bear out to blow off some steam. Then I saw you were home"—he cocked his head at the truck—"and thought I'd say hello." His dark brows furrowed together. "What's the matter?"

"Nothing."

Damon crossed his arms over his chest. "Your face and your bear say otherwise. Where's Dutchy?"

He couldn't stop the growl coming from his throat.

"Ah." Damon stepped closer. "Mate troubles. Want to talk about it?"

"No."

The chief sat down beside him. "When you guys

disappeared the other night, I thought you'd worked things out. What happened since then?"

He wanted to tell Damon to fuck off and leave him alone so he could wallow in self-pity. But he knew better than to try and shake him off. Goddamn Damon was like a dog with a bone when he set his mind on something. Relentless. Unflagging. It was no wonder he'd risen up the ranks in the army so quickly.

"Fuck. I don't know." He raked his hand through his hair and relayed to him what had happened. "And ... Goddammit, I don't know why the hell she wants to know about that shit." His stomach turned to ice just thinking about the two innocent lives he'd taken.

Damon didn't say anything for a while, just sat quietly next to him. "Krieg," he finally began. "Remember what I told you a couple months back? About asking forgiveness of ourselves?"

He closed his eyes. "Yeah. Of course I do."

Sometimes ... sometimes we have to ask forgiveness of ourselves.

"And have you?

"Yeah."

"Really?"

Krieger huffed. "I know I wasn't to blame for our guys getting killed. You said it yourself. And I understand, it was war. We had bad intelligence."

"But what about after? Those two farmers from the village—"

"No!" he roared. "Stop." They *never* talked about that.

"Krieger, it's obvious that's what's been hurting you this whole time."

"I'm better. I've changed. Why isn't that enough?" *Why am I not enough for her?*

"You can't just change overnight, Krieg. Even with me, it took a while. It took professional help, six months of therapy.

And I'm still not one hundred percent. Recovery … it's a process, not just a one-and-done thing. Maybe … maybe it's time you let others handle the burden for you for a bit."

"Whaddaya mean?"

"Like the guys said that night, we want to help you." A hand landed on his shoulder and squeezed. "Since I started coming here, you've always let me talk and ramble on. You've been watching me—all of us, really—over these past couple of months. And you've been trying to make yourself into a better person. It's a lot to juggle and deal with. So why not let us carry the burden for a bit? Lean on your friends. Lean on me."

"I … I don't know how."

A smile spread across Damon's face. "How about we do it like we always do? Start with a beer? And then we can just … talk and go from there?"

Krieger sighed. "All right."

Chapter 16

"Well, spank my ass and call me Sally!" J.D. chortled as she rounded the bend up the steep mountain road. "Tim and Angela, really? And you walked in on them doing the nasty?"

"Don't remind me," Dutchy groaned. "It was a miracle I was able to look them both in the eye throughout that dinner." Of course, a reminder of last night only brought back the dark cloud she'd been fighting.

"Stop that."

"Stop what?"

"Stop looking like the world is over," J.D. said. "It's not. You're going to show up at his cabin and tell him you're sorry. He's going to be so happy to see you, and he'll ask for your forgiveness for being a jackass."

"He wasn't being a jackass."

"He was being presumptuous, thinking he could fix you. News flash, Dutchy: You're already awesome. Plus, that comment about Ian was a low blow, and you didn't deserve that. So don't you let him walk over you like a doormat either, okay?"

Dutchy couldn't help the smile on her face. "I'm really glad you're here, J.D. I mean ... I know you and I weren't friends in the beginning and we just were kind of tossed together when everyone found their mates. But ... I'm glad to call you my friend."

"Awww ... now you're going to make *me* cry."

"I promise not to ignore you if Krieger and I ever work it out."

"You mean, *when*," J.D. corrected. "And Dutchy, it's all right. I totally understand. That's just how things are, you know? You find your mate, then the kids arrive, and they come first. I'm happy to be the cool aunt on the sidelines who gets to spoil all the babies and then hand them back to their parents when they start crying while I kick back in my bachelor pad."

She grinned gratefully at J.D. While she may be tough on the outside, Dutchy always knew J.D. had a soft inside. She only hoped that the blonde mechanic could find someone—mate or not—who could handle all that and deserve her.

"Say, Dutchy" J.D.'s delicate nose wrinkled. "Are we almost there yet?"

She peeked out the window. They'd been driving over an hour and half by now, and the road signs said they were approaching Contessa Peak. If she remembered what Krieger had told her correctly, the main road should lead to a parking lot on the other side where most day hikers started their journey. But the dirt road to his cabin split off before then. "We need to get off the highway soon. Should be up ahead."

A few miles later, Dutchy spotted the turnoff. "There. Slow down ... yeah, through here."

J.D. maneuvered the vehicle onto the dirt road and they rumbled along. "Wow, this really is a long way up," J.D. said. "I don't think I've been this far up the mountains."

"Do you go to the mountains a lot?"

"When I was young, with my old man," J.D. said. "We used

to love to go out and hunt together, but we never made it up here. Our animals prefer flatlands and dry climates."

Dutchy held her tongue, trying not to ask the question on her mind. She'd always wondered what J.D. was exactly, but never did ask because, well, that was rude in the shifter world. However, from the scent of fur, she could at least tell J.D. was some sort of feline. But what kind of cat specifically liked flat lands and dry heat? Lionesses? Cougars?

"There was this one time—whoa!"

They bounced up so violently that her teeth rattled in her brain. J.D. slammed on the brakes. "What the fuck—did we run over a dragon's turd or something?" The car then began to slide back. "Oh crap!" The engine roared as she pressed on the gas, but they didn't move. "Fuck!" Taking her seatbelt off, J.D. got out of the car.

Dutchy unbuckled her belt and slipped out. "J.D.?"

The blonde mechanic squatted down near the back of the car. "Aww shit. Looks like it rained a lot last night. Washed out the dirt and left that big boulder sticking out. And now the tires are stuck in the mud."

Walking over to her, Dutchy bent down next to J.D. The rear tires were, indeed, mired down deeply in a mix of mud and wet leaves. "Could we get it out?"

"We could try."

And so, they did, with J.D. in the back pushing while Dutchy attempted to drive it out. The tires spun and spun, and the engine roared and sputtered, but the car didn't budge.

"Fuck." J.D. cursed as she kicked the tires and wiped the mud from her jeans. She'd also lost her hat at some point, and her wild mop of blonde curls stuck out from her head. "Sorry, Dutchy. Your tires just weren't made for this."

Dutchy sighed. What else could possibly go wrong today?

"Hey, none of that now," J.D. admonished. "You said this

dirt road lead up to his cabin, right? We're both young and healthy, we can make it up there."

She glanced up at the road ahead. J.D. was right. It wasn't the end of the world just because her car was stuck in the mud. "All right, I guess we should start walking."

J.D. scraped off as much of the mud as she could, then they began to trudge up the road.

"Sorry you had to get stuck up here with me," Dutchy began. "And that you got all dirty."

"Nah, don't worry about it," J.D. said with a wave. "I was never afraid of a little dirt."

They continued their walk up without speaking much. It felt like they had been going for a long time, yet there was no cabin in sight. Had they taken a wrong turn, or was it farther than she thought?

"Are we there yet?" J.D. asked.

"I think—"

A shriek from somewhere deep in the woods made them both freeze. "What the hell was that?" J.D. swung her head around.

"I don't know. But I don't like the sound of that scream."

"Me neither." J.D.'s brows furrowed.

"A lost hiker, maybe?"

"The rangers should—"

Another ear-piercing cry rang through the air. Goosebumps rose all over Dutchy's arms. "Oh. God."

J.D. let out a hiss. "We should at least check it out. If someone fell and hurt themselves, they might need help sooner than later."

Dutchy glanced up the road, feeling torn. But J.D. was right. Someone could be hurt bad, and she'd never be able to sleep at night if that person was in need when she could have done something about it. "All right. Let's go."

"I think it came from that way," J.D. cocked her head into the line of trees. "I can hear them ... follow me."

Dutchy focused her sensitive hearing. She could hear some faint rustling sounds from deep in the forest, but being feline, J.D.'s ears were much more sensitive, so she walked ahead. As they made their way through the thicket, she could hear more sounds—shuffling feet and voices.

Suddenly, J.D. held up a hand, then turned to her, put her finger over her lips, then motioned for her to get lower on the ground.

They crouched low and waddled forward, slowly approaching the source of the noise which came from behind a low ridge. Peering over the top of the ridge, Dutchy bit her lip to prevent the gasp from escaping her lips.

"... think we used enough tranqs?"

"Yeah. She's a tiny thing, shouldn't need much."

Two men wearing forest fatigues stood over a small heap on the ground. Focusing her vision, Dutchy could see that it was a small doe. One of them knelt down beside it and tied its front and rear legs together, then hauled the doe up onto his shoulders. "C'mon, let's get her in the cage before she wakes up and shifts back."

Dutchy opened her mouth in outrage, but J.D. slapped a hand over it, sending her a warning glare. They didn't move for what seemed like an eternity. Finally, J.D. loosened her hand. "They should be far away enough," she said. "But stay quiet, okay?"

Dutchy nodded, and J.D. released her. "Oh God. That poor doe ... those men ... how did they even get up here?"

"I don't know." J.D.'s light hazel eyes burned, and Dutchy could feel her animal's rage. Her fox, too, was fueled by J.D.'s anger and let out a hiss. "We need to rescue her."

"But ... but shouldn't we get help?"

"It might be too late," J.D. pointed out. "Who knows what they'll do to her by the time we can reach Krieger's cabin or if we can even find help."

Her fox nodded and agreed.

"Let's at least follow them and see what they're up to. If they have some kind of transport, we can take down the make, model, and tags, then report them to the rangers."

"Krieger has a radio in his cabin," Dutchy said. "He can call it in. They'll catch them before they can even get off the mountain."

"All right, let's go. They went ..." J.D. closed her eyes as she focused her senses. "This way."

Her heart thumped as she followed J.D. though the woods. How she managed to stay calm and collected as they tracked the men, Dutchy didn't know, but she admired her friend's nerves of steel.

They continued to follow them, going deeper into the forest. Where they were, she didn't know, but it didn't seem like they were anywhere near a road where someone could park any type of getaway vehicle.

J.D. halted all of a sudden, then crouched low, pulling her down. "Holy crap. Over there."

The men had reappeared through the thicket of trees, then headed toward a solid, jagged wall covered in moss, seemingly melting right into the rock.

Dutchy frowned. "Where did they go?"

"Hmmm ..." J.D. worried at her lower lip. "Might be a cave, let's take a closer look."

As they drew nearer to the wall, Dutchy's nose picked up a powerful odor. "Oh God, what the hell is that?"

J.D. lifted her head and took a sniff. "Ugh. Smells like bear." She opened her mouth, flicked up her tongue, and then grimaced. "Definitely bear ... but it seems ... wrong."

"Wrong?"

"Yeah. Bears—both shifter and real ones—have unique scents. For real bears, I can usually tell if it's a different species. But this ... it's like a bunch of different bears had some kind of wild orgy and rubbed themselves all over the place." Her eyes narrowed. "That, or it's a manufactured scent."

"A fake bear scent? Why would anyone spread that here?"

J.D.'s expression darkened. "To throw off anyone that might get too curious."

Her heart leapt into her throat. "Oh God."

"I'll bet there *is* some kind of cave hidden back there," J.D. said. "We should go in and investigate."

"What? No!" She grabbed J.D.'s arm and pulled her back down. "What if there's more of them? We can't go in there by ourselves. Let's go back and get help."

J.D. hesitated as she glanced back toward where the men had disappeared with the doe shifter. "What if ..." She huffed. "All right. I mean, you're right. If we can make it to Krieger's cabin, he can call for backup." She stood upright and brushed the dirt and leaves from her pants legs. "If we—yeow!" she yelped as she slapped her left hand over her other arm.

"What's the matter?"

J.D. yanked something out of her arm that looked like a long silver tube with a pink pompom at the end. "Dutch ..."

"What—J.D.!" J.D.'s eyes rolled back, and her body fell forward. Dutchy lunged to catch her, but something hit her in the back, making her double over. Her face hit the ground, and pain bloomed in her cheek. Planting her palms down, she pushed herself up, but her limbs weakened, and she fell down again.

Footsteps drew nearer, and panic rose in her as her fox's hackles raised and urged her to get up. Though she wanted to move, her body protested. Exhaustion seeped in, and she could barely keep her eyes open.

As she drifted in and out of consciousness, she wasn't sure if the things she could hear and feel were real. There was a sensation of floating—or was she being lifted up? Harsh, angry voices rang around her. Then she was thrown down and dragged across something cold and wet. Finally, there was a sound of metal clanging and a heavy clicking sound before everything went silent.

Her body fought and fought. It was like swimming for hours in thick syrup. But at some point, she took a deep gulp and opened her eyes. Her vision was still blurry but slowly adjusted to the darkness as sensation returned to her limbs. Her body tensed, but when she opened her mouth, a small hand grasped over hers. She took a sniff, and the scent of familiar fur filled her nostrils. *J.D.!*

Slowly, her eyes focused. She was lying on her side, face to face with J.D. Her eyes were open wide, and her hand squeezed hers tight. Understanding that she wanted her to keep playing possum, she gave her hand a squeeze back and closed her eyes.

A light flickered on overhead. Footsteps closed in on them, and she could feel their presence right over them, staring down.

"... what the fuck are these two broads doing up here anyway?" the first man replied. "I thought we were far away from the trails?"

"Maybe they got lost," a third man said. "Why the fuck did you shoot them, Gordon? They might have just gone away."

"And what if they didn't, huh?" the second man—Gordon, apparently—spat back. "What if they saw enough of our little operation here and ran back to those fucking rangers? It'll be months of work down the drain, and we haven't broken even yet. You gonna tell our investors we can't pay back their money, Turner?"

"Fuck. I didn't spend months living in a cave covered in bear shit for nothin'," Turner cursed. "Joey—how many have we caught and shipped? Three now?"

"Yeah. Four if you count the doe," Joey replied. "That's five grand each."

"Minus expenses, and we're still in the hole," Gordon replied. "Shifter-proofing those doors ain't cheap, ya know."

Turner spat. "But what are we gonna do about those bitches? We can't smuggle them down in our backpacks. That doe alone will be hard to hide if we come across any rangers."

Gordon huffed. "Tranqs should last until morning. Even if they wake up, they won't be able to escape. We'll deal with them tomorrow. C'mon, let's eat, I'm fucking starved. "

"Me too," Turner said with a laugh. "Hunting down these animals is enough to give me an appetite. Let's lock 'em up and get outta here."

The sound of heavy footsteps echoed away from them, followed by the sound of metal scraping against stone. When the silence finally settled over them, Dutchy opened her eyes, her vision slowly adjusting to the darkness. "Did you hear—"

"Yeah." J.D.'s face was twisted in rage. "Those bastards." Her voice trembled. "We can't let them get away with this."

"They think we're human," Dutchy said.

"Good." J.D. braced her palms down and pushed herself up. She sniffed the air. "It smells ... damp. We must be in a cave of some sort."

The rock under her hands as she struggled to get up said as much.

J.D. helped her up. "Are you okay? You—Look!" She pointed to the wooden beams above them.

"What are those?"

"Supports. I know what this is!" She snapped her fingers. "It's an old mine. For blackstone." The Blackstone Mountains were named for the hardest mineral on earth—which could only be found here and mined using dragon fire. It was what made the Lennoxes one of the richest families on earth. "I bet this was one of the earlier sites Lucas Lennox mined when he first discovered the blackstone. I wouldn't be surprised if he just abandoned it when the deposits dried up and no one's been here for decades. Those guys must have found it."

"And now it's some sort of hideout for what ... a poaching scheme?"

"Poaching for shifters," J.D. concluded. "Goddamn bastards! I'm going to tear their throats out then feed whatever's left to Matthew and Jason Lennox!"

"What do we do, J.D.? They said they'd take care of us in the morning." Dutchy could guess what they mean by that.

J.D. put on a determined face. "Not gonna happen. We're gonna have to find a way out."

"There's light coming from that way," Dutchy pointed out. "But that's probably where those poachers went."

"Let's try the other way first, then. C'mon."

They walked along the cramped mine shaft, using one side of the wall as a guide. However, they didn't get very far and ended up at a solid stone wall.

"Dead end," Dutchy guessed.

J.D. put her ear to the wall. "Solid all the way through. Let's see what the other way is like."

Turning around, they ambled in the opposite direction. When they reached the end, it was blocked by something solid, but a small shaft of light poured through a gap underneath.

"Steel," Dutchy said as she touched the obstruction. "I don't think we'll be able to move this out of the way, even if we worked together. And they said it was shifter proof."

"Huh." J.D. knelt down and pushed her hand under the gap. "All right, I'm gonna break us out of here."

"You are? How?"

She stretched her neck and rolled her shoulders. "How else? I'm going to shift."

"Into your animal?"

"Exactly." A smile spread over her face. "I'll have us out of here in no time."

What was J.D.'s plan? Was her animal *that* huge that its bulk would break through metal? "Maybe you should take your clothes off first?"

"No need." J.D. opened her mouth and let out a sharp hiss as her incisors elongated. Fur popped up on her face. Dutchy scooted away, closing her eyes to give J.D. some privacy. She waited for a deep roar. For powerful paws to slam on the ground. To her surprise, nothing happened. "Huh?" Opening her eyes, the only thing she saw was a heap of J.D.'s clothing in front of her. "What the—"

A small bump moved around from under J.D.'s shirt. It wiggled and twitched until something popped up from the neck —a small, feline head with tawny fur, a brown nose with white whiskers, and huge, light hazel eyes.

Dutchy blinked. "J.D.? You're a cat?"

The animal hissed at her and shook its head.

Well, you sure look like a cat, she thought silently. J.D.'s animal—whatever it was—was about the size of a small domesticated cat. As it emerged from the pile of clothes, she could see the rest of its body was covered in irregular black spots, while stripes ringed around its neck and legs. It was such an unusual coloring for a cat, plus its tail was much shorter too.

J.D.'s animal sniffed around the bottom of the steel door. Flattening itself, the feline pushed its head through the small gap, then squirmed out.

Hope soared through her chest. "You did it!" Dutchy exclaimed. "That was amazing! Er ... what are you?"

"No time to explain." J.D. said through the door. "Shit!"

"What's wrong?"

"This door ... it's built right into the stone. And there's a lock. Fuck!"

Her stomach sank. "J.D. ... you have to go."

"Go? I can't leave you! I'll find the key and—"

"There's no time," she whispered. "They could come back and find you. Please. I'll be fine."

"If they realize I'm gone and you're still here—"

"They won't," she insisted. "They said they won't check on us until morning. You'll be able to head back and get help by then."

"But—"

"Please, J.D.! You know it's the only way."

The silence from the other side of the door lasted for a few heartbeats. "All right. You hang on tight, Dutchy. I'll get help and come back for you."

"I know you will."

"And when I come and rescue you, we can go have drinks in The Den." She could almost see J.D.'s smile. "You're part of a very special club now."

"I am?"

"Yeah," she said with a chuckle. "The only ones who know that I'm a—"

"You can tell me later. At The Den," she said. "Now *go*."

"All righty. Sit tight, Dutch. I'll bring the cavalry."

"See you, J.D."

Dutchy sank down to the ground and hugged her knees to herself. *Oh God, please don't let them come back before J.D. gets help.*

Those men ... she couldn't believe they'd been hiding out here the entire time. And what for? Hunting down shifters and selling them? To whom? She shuddered to think of the fates of those three others they had already succeeded in capturing. And what they might do to her in the morning.

J.D. would come back with help. But then, the mountains were huge, and J.D. had never been this far up before. *I have to be ready.* She'd never had to fight before—but as a fox, she'd done plenty of play fighting with the other kits in her skulk.

Her vixen relished the idea of a fight as it licked its lips. She may not be a bear or a wolf or another apex predator, but she had bite. *I'm not giving up so easily.* No, not when she now had so much to live for. Her mate. She would go to Krieger, apologize for what happened, and tell him she loved him.

Chapter 17

Krieger had never been the type of talk about his feelings with anyone. When Damon first started visiting him, it was mostly his former commander who did the talking. Krieger hadn't felt the need to open up, but Damon's presence and friendship had inspired him to change. And now, maybe the chief was right. It was time for him to lighten his burden.

"If she found out what happened ... what I did to those two innocent men, she'll never look at me the same way," he said. Seeing as Damon didn't have to go back home until after dinner, they cooked a couple of steaks and then sat out on the now-darkened porch, drinking the last of the beers from the fridge.

"She's your mate," Damon says. "She'll understand."

"But what if she doesn't? What if she hates me?"

Damon put his can down. "That's what I thought would happen if Anna Victoria found out about ... about what I did." Damon had confessed to him about how he had lost control of his bear during a romp with some base bunny after he thought he was 'cured' from his PTSD. "So, I pushed my mate away, convinced that I was no good for her. But you know what? She wouldn't accept that. She fought me tooth and nail and wore me down." He chuckled.

"But this is different ... there's no denying I killed two innocent people."

"Who were hunting you down for *sport*," Damon reminded him. "They knew the consequences of tangling with a wild animal."

"But—"

"Krieg. *John*." Damon's tone was firmer now. "Dutchy is your mate. If she feels anything for you, she'll understand and accept you for who you are now and what happened in your past. And if she doesn't, then maybe you guys shouldn't be together. The mating bond will never form if you're not fully open and fully committed."

His heart thudded in his chest. The thought of not being with Dutchy made something ache in him, but then they might not even have a chance if she rejected him after finding out what a monster he was. "I—"

His bear's hackles rising made him stop short. Damon, too, must have sensed the presence approaching them, and he shot to his feet. Something was out there in the darkness.

A small, glowing green orb floated in the darkness, coming closer until a four-legged creature padded out into the light. The grizzled, one-eyed wolf moved closer, slowly turning into its human form.

"Milos." Damon relaxed and so did Krieger. "You're out late. Care to join us? We don't have any beer left, though."

Milos shook his head. "That is not why I'm here."

Krieger immediately noticed the tension in the wolf shifter's stance. "What's wrong?"

"I found a vehicle down the road, stuck in the mud and abandoned."

"I didn't see any car when I drove up," Krieger said. "Must have come after me."

"If the car's stuck, maybe they went back down to get help," Damon guessed. "Did you see anyone?"

Milos shook his head. "No, I think it has been a few hours." He frowned. "I must tell you something, Chief. What I've discovered."

"About what?" Damon asked. "Did you find the missing raccoon shifter?"

"No. But I did find something else."

"What?"

"Patterns. Others who may have disappeared. I asked Petros to check if there are other shifters who have been reported missing in the last few weeks. It turns out there were: an older man, Julius MacKenna, a raven shifter who works as a mechanic in town and a female rabbit shifter named Bridgette Smythe."

"So, you think all of them are connected?" Damon asked. "And this car down the road, what about it?"

"I've noticed strange movements in the forest. Smells that should not be there. Tracks that seem abnormal. I've been trying to follow the trail, but it keeps eluding me. I am not sure if the abandoned car is connected, but it seems a strange coincidence." Milos's nose wrinkled. "But perhaps we should investigate?"

"I'll come with you," Krieger volunteered.

The three men trudged down the muddy road. About four or five miles down, Krieger spied the blue Honda, stopped at an angle off the trail, as if it had slid down. Rounding to the back, he bent down and inspected the tires. Just as Milos described, it was stuck deep in the mud. But that wasn't what caught his eye. A few feet away was a trucker cap, half-buried in the mud. Picking it up, he brushed the dirt from the front, revealing a logo that read "J.D.'s Garage."

"Chief!" he shouted. "You need to see this."

"What is it?" Damon asked he scrambled over. Krieger stood up and showed him the cap. "That's J.D.'s."

"Found it in the mud."

Damon's jaw hardened. "This isn't her car," he said through gritted teeth. "She drives a mint green classic Ford truck."

"Then whose car is it?" Milos asked.

Damon tucked the cap into his back jeans pocket. "Let's find out."

They walked up to the front doors. Krieger was the first to reach the passenger side, so he yanked it open and stuck his head inside. The familiar scent hit him right away. "Fuck!" Reaching for the glovebox, he pulled it open and grabbed the paperwork inside. Sure enough, the registration said the owner was Duchess Marie Forrester. "Motherfucker!"

"Krieger?" Damon asked as he stuck his head in from the driver's side. "Whose car is it?"

"Dutchy's."

"Dutchy? But how?"

Blood roared in his ears as his bear reared up. Something was definitely wrong. What could have happened? *Think.* "This morning, she—" Then he remembered. "J.D. had her car. Fixed up a leak for her and rotated her tires, then was going to bring it by this morning." This morning. After their huge blowup. And now ...

"Krieg? You all right?"

She'd been so mad at him.

Asked him to leave.

But why was her car here?

He swallowed hard, ice forming in his stomach. "She came up here ... to see me." Despite his hurtful words and his refusal to open up to her, she was coming to him. But she never made it.

"Where is she, then?" Milos asked. "Why would she come up here to see you, then abandon her car when she got stuck?

Couldn't she have walked up the road to your cabin? From the faintness of their scents, they've been gone for hours."

"I don't know." Krieger curled his fingers into fists. "But I'm gonna find out." And if someone had taken her—hurt her—they were going to pay.

"I'm gonna call HQ," Damon said. "Have them call her or her aunts to see if she's made it back. J.D., too."

"You do that," Krieger said. "But I'm gonna search the area."

"I shall join you as well," Milos said.

"I—fine, I'm not gonna argue," Damon said, resigned. "If it were Anna Victoria, I'd do the same. Stay safe, and if you find anything you can't handle, come back. We'll call for—"

A loud rustling made all three men tense up. They looked at each in silent communication, their animals ready for a fight as they all turned toward the direction of the sound. Slowly, they crept toward the bushes, watching and waiting for whatever would come out.

Meow!

A small, furry ball leapt out from the foliage, headed straight for Damon. "What—oh hey!" The chief easily caught the creature. "It's you," he said, chuckling. He lifted the thing up and stared into its face. "I was so worried about you. Where have you been?"

"Damon?" Krieger frowned. "You know this"—he squinted at the thing as it was so tiny—"cat?"

The creature glared at him, light hazel eyes flashing, then let out a hiss.

"Shh ... don't be like that," Damon tucked the fur ball into the crook of his arm. "Sorry. She's sensitive about her animal."

"Who's sensitive?" Krieger exclaimed, losing his patience.

"This is—ow!" Damon cried out as the cat dug its claws into his arm. "Well, if you're going to be like that, fine." Placing the cat on the ground, he took his shirt off and lay it next to the creature. "Turn around," he ordered Milos and Krieger.

"But—"

"Just do it, okay?"

Milos and Krieger looked at each other, shrugged, and did as Damon asked. Seconds later, a familiar voice broke the silence of the night.

"Krieger, you overgrown teddy bear!" J.D. screamed. "How dare you call me a fucking cat!"

Whirling around, he stared at her, not quite believing it, even though he'd seen it.

"Now, now, J.D.," Damon began. "You know not everyone knows what you are."

"What *are* you then?" Krieger asked. *Because she sure looked like a fucking cat.*

"FYI"—J.D., dressed only in Damon's shirt that came down to her knees, sauntered over to him, hand on her hips—"my animal is *felis nigripes*. Also known as—"

"The African black-footed cat," Milos finished.

"Thank you," J.D. said with a grateful nod.

"So ... you *are* a cat," Krieger concluded.

J.D.'s face twisted in annoyance, and she let out a snarl. "Don't you know anything? My animal is the deadliest feline in the world. Sixty percent success rate, averaging ten to fifteen prey a night. That's one every fifty minutes."

"One what? Cricket?"

"Why you—" J.D. leapt at him, but Damon quickly wrapped his arm around her waist and swung her back.

"J.D.," Damon warned. "Stop. What the hell are you doing up here prowling around in your animal form anyway? And where's Dutchy?"

J.D. stopped struggling and wrenched herself from Damon's

arms. "Fuck! Sorry. Got distracted." She lifted her head up to meet Krieger's eyes. "They have her locked up."

"Who?" Krieger's voice boomed as rage tore through him. "Who has her?"

J.D. quickly recounted what happened to them and what they had discovered about the poachers, confirming Milos's theory that the disappearances were indeed connected. "I tried to get her out," she said with a sniff. "But the door was locked and too heavy. She said I needed to come here and get help."

"Goddammit, I'm gonna kill all of them if they hurt her," Krieger growled. His bear, too, roared in agreement.

"We should call for backup," Damon said.

Krieger shook his head. "If there's only three of them and three of us—"

"*Ahem*," J.D. cleared her throat and raised a brown at him.

"*Four* of us," he corrected. "We can take them on. Please, Damon, there's no time to waste."

"We should at least assess the situation," Milos said. "And see if it would be viable for us to attack and rescue the female or retreat and call for assistance."

"The abandoned mine's not too far," J.D. said. "About ... a mile or so up the ridge."

"I ... all right," Damon relented. "Let's go."

Krieger knew there wouldn't be any retreat, but he was glad for the wolf shifter's suggestion. They followed J.D., who remained in human form, as she led them toward the abandoned mine. As they drew nearer, Krieger could barely contain the seething anger building inside him. *We'll find her*, he assured his bear, who was already raring to unleash its power. *And then we'll make those men pay.*

"There." J.D. pointed out the entrance to the mine. "In there."

"We should check the perimeter for—Krieger!"

No way was he waiting around while his mate was locked up in there with three fucking shifter poachers who were going to kill her by morning. He bolted towards the mine, his bear ripping out of him. The humongous grizzly barely fit though the entrance, but it barreled in anyway. The roar that ripped from its throat reverberated through the narrow chambers, announcing his presence.

Alarmed cries drifted in from the shaft on the right, followed by the shuffling of feet. The bear rushed toward that direction, its massive body filling the tiny space.

"What the hel—"

"It's a fucking bear!"

"Grab the tranqs!"

The mighty grizzly charged forward, catching one man with its left paw. The claws ripped through skin and flesh like tissue paper, and the man's blood-curdling scream echoed down the chamber. Getting down on all fours, the bear chased the remaining men down the narrow tunnel. Another scream pierced the air as the bear swiped its claws down the second man's head. It barely stopped, rushing forward as it hunted down its final prey. But the third human was gone. Where did he go?

"Motherfucker!"

The man reappeared behind him from an antechamber the bear hadn't noticed. He raised something in his hands—a long-barreled rifle. "Eat lead, monster!"

Everything happened in an instant. The bear roared and charged forward. A scream of pain. A gunshot. Krieger thought they'd been shot but felt no pain on their body.

"Goddammit, Krieger! I told you to wait."

As the adrenaline seeped from his veins, Krieger's vision cleared. The man holding the gun was on the floor, blood seeping out from his jugular as the one-eyed wolf stood over him, muzzle dripping with blood. Damon stood behind the wolf, eyeing the grizzly disapprovingly.

"What the—Jesus titty-fucking Christ!" J.D. exclaimed when she saw the bloodbath. "You—wait!" She crawled over to the man on the ground and reached for something on his waist. "Yes!" She raised her hand triumphantly, shaking a set of keys on a ring. "Let's go get your mate," she said to Krieger, then turned around and disappeared down the tunnel.

By the time he caught up to J.D., he had already shifted into his human form. A pit formed in his stomach as various scenarios ran through his head. Had they discovered J.D. had gone? Did they retaliate by turning on Dutchy? If something had happened to her, he'd never forgive himself.

"I unlocked it, but the door's too heavy—hey!"

Krieger pulled the female away from the door, grabbed the handle, and pulled it open. "Dutchy? Are you—"

A loud *yip* echoed through the air, and a small, red furry ball leapt out from the darkness. Thanks to his shifter senses, he managed to catch the fox in his arms. "Dutchy!" He didn't care if the fox was protesting at being held in his arms or that its claws were ripping at him. He needed to hold her. To know she was okay.

"Uh, Krieger?" Damon said. "Maybe you should, uh, let go." He nodded at the blood dripping down his arms.

Krieger put the little fox down. "All right, you got what you wanted," he said to the creature, showing it the wounds on his arms. "Can I have her back now, please?"

The fox did an indignant little twirl, then settled down, before its limbs began to grow and fur disappeared into skin. "John!" Dutchy cried as she leapt into his arms. "You came for me."

"Of course I did," he said, eagerly lifting her to him. He

ALICIA MONTGOMERY

pushed his nose into the crook of her neck, inhaling her scent, which calmed his bear down. She was here. She was safe.

"John, I'm—"

Damon cleared his throat. "If you guys don't mind ... maybe we should get out of here? Call for the authorities?"

"Oh my God, I almost forgot!" Dutchy slapped her palm over her forehead. "There was a doe shifter. And the poachers! What if they've hurt her? We need—"

"Shh ..." Krieger soothed, running a hand down her smooth back. "The poachers won't hurt her. They won't hurt anyone anymore."

"But we should find the doe," J.D. said.

"I'll head back to your cabin and call HQ," Damon said. "You guys find the missing shifter, and maybe see if there are others in here who need help."

Krieger wanted to be alone with Dutchy, to tell her so many things and kiss her and hold her. However, when his mate turned to him, her blue eyes filled with joy and understanding, he knew what she was trying to say. That there would be time enough for that. *Later then*, he thought. "All right, Chief," he said to Damon. "We'll get right on it."

———

The doe shifter was quickly found, deeper inside the abandoned mine in another locked antechamber similar to the one where Dutchy and J.D. had been kept. The young woman, whose name was Hannah, was shaken and dehydrated, but otherwise, she was fine. Apparently, she'd been exploring the woods when the two poachers came upon her and shot her with a tranquilizer.

Backup came not too long after that. Anders and Daniel had both been working the night shift, and so they rushed to

Contessa Peak right away. However, they were not the only ones who responded. Jason Lennox arrived with a team of his own from the Shifter Protection Agency—or The Agency—a secret task force that worked to protect their kind where law enforcement and the government fell short.

J.D. and Dutchy relayed to Jason what they had overheard, that the poachers had found the abandoned mine, used it as their base in the mountains so they could hunt down unsuspecting shifters, then sneak them off so they could be sold.

The dragon shifter, of course, was not happy to hear that poachers had been operating right under their noses, here in the most sacred of his family's territory. "We'll figure out everyone who's connected to them, where they are, and take them down," Jason vowed. "And find those missing shifters they sold."

The night dragged on as the agents took all their statements, gathered evidence, and catalogued everything. Krieger and Damon also insisted that J.D. and Dutchy be checked out by the medic from the Agency to make sure they were okay. Dutchy had lost her cast when she shifted, but then her arm seemed fine anyway, so they didn't need to re-cast it.

A couple of hours later, Jason informed them they could leave and promised to get in touch when they found the missing shifters.

"Thanks, Jason," J.D. said, her voice trembling. "Julius ... he was one of my most reliable mechanics. I should have known something was up when he just didn't show up. I just never thought—"

"You couldn't have known," Dutchy said, giving her a side-hug. "No one could. And Bridgette was the same. Aunt Rosie just thought she'd found another job."

"It's been a long night," Damon declared. "I'm gonna get a ride with Daniel back to HQ. How about you, J.D.?"

"Yeah, I'll come with." The feline shifter turned to Dutchy. "You riding with us?"

She smiled shyly up at Krieger. "I ... I don't think I'll need a ride."

No, she definitely did not. "I'll take her back," he said.

They said their goodbyes, then Damon and J.D. got into the transport truck with Daniel and Anders and drove off. Finally, they were alone.

"Let's take a walk," Krieger said, offering her his hand.

"Yes," she replied, taking it. The warmth of her skin sent a tingle up his arm, all the way to his chest.

They walked back to his cabin in silence, and Krieger was glad for the cool autumn air that cleared away the scent of blood and death. Arriving at his cabin, they climbed up the porch, hand in hand, their steps in synch.

A howl came in from the distance, breaking the silence.

"What—"

"Milos," Krieger explained. "Probably out patrolling."

Dutchy's nose twitched. "So, what's up with him?" she asked. "What's he doing up here?"

"I'm not sure," he replied. "But whatever it is ... I think he's working through it." And he hoped, that someday, the wolf shifter would be able to conquer his demons. "So, uh, would you like to come in?"

"Yes."

Pushing the door open, he let her go inside first. "Dutchy, I—"

"No." She held a hand up. "Let me go first."

"Okay."

"I'm sorry. I'm so sorry, John, for blowing up at you this morning. For thinking the worst of you when you were only trying to help." Her expression was one of true remorse.

"You don't have to say sorry," he said. "I overstepped my

bounds. Invaded your privacy. And I ... I shouldn't have said that about that man in the picture with you."

"Oh, John, you don't have to worry about him."

"I know. You had a life before you met me. I was being insecure and hurt. You're right. I should stop trying to fix you. You don't have to be fixed, Dutchy. You're wonderful and perfect, just the way you are."

She smiled shyly at him. "I am?"

"Uh-huh. And I meant what I said. I'll take care of you. Whatever you want to do, I'll support you."

"Really?"

"Yeah."

"And if I never design again?"

"Then you can do whatever you want. Be what you want to be."

"Like what?"

"Anything." He took her hands and wrapped them in his. "Anything your heart wants. Be a dancer. A singer. Lawyer. Taxidermist."

She giggled. "I don't know if taxidermists are in demand in Blackstone. What would I do for money?"

"You wouldn't need to worry about that," he said. "I'd take care of you. You can stay home with the cubs and—" He stopped short, realizing what he just said. But the thought of it —Dutchy carrying his cubs, her belly growing round, made something primal in him rejoice. Her silence, however, planted a seed of doubt in his gut. "I didn't mean ... if you ... we don't—"

"Kits."

"What?"

Tears gathered at the corners of her pale blue eyes. "Foxes ... have kits."

"Oh. Of course," he swallowed hard.

"But I'd like at least one of each," she finished. "One kit and one cub. To start, anyway."

He sucked in a breath. "Dutchy—"

Her hands reached up and pulled him down for a kiss. Happiness, relief, pure joy, burst from his chest as their mouths melded. Her sweet taste burst on his tongue, like tasting the first sun-ripened berries in the summer. Heat and desire curled in his belly, but more than that, something else stirred inside him. Emotion. True emotions he never thought he'd ever feel. "I love you, Dutchy," he breathed against her lips.

"John ..." She kissed him deep. "I lov—"

"Wait."

"What's wrong?"

It pained him to stop her, but he couldn't let her say the words without fully knowing the truth about him. "Before you continue ... I need to tell you something." His heart pounded in his chest, and he could only pray that Damon was right.

Chapter 18

"John?" Dutchy peered up at him. "John, what's the matter?" Did he not want her to say the words? To return the love she could clearly see in his eyes and feel in her bones?

"You were right, Dutchy," he began. "About me keeping things from you. I didn't want to tell you the truth because I thought you would hate me—"

"I could never—"

"Please, Dutchy." He grabbed her hands and kissed her palms. "Wait. And listen. And then decide if I'm worthy of you."

How could he even think he wasn't worthy? After all this time and all the things he did to be with her? For her? "All right. Tell me."

Taking her hand in his, he pulled her to the leather chair in the corner, sat her down, and knelt in front of her. "When I was in the Special Forces, my commander—Damon—sent me and my team into a market building...."

The pain in his eyes was evident as he recounted the events

that led to the deaths of his team members and how seeking out justice for them took its toll on him. She wanted to reach out and take all that away. To comfort him and make everything right.

"I'm sorry for what you went through," she said, cupping his face. "But you did what you had to do. For your friends who were killed and so those terrorists could never hurt anyone again."

"There's more," he said, his voice cracking unnaturally. "After that ... I couldn't control my bear. It wanted more blood, more violence. So, I hid out in the mountains, staying far away from anyone who I could hurt. But it didn't last too long. And I ... I killed again."

"What happened?" Though dread pooled in her gut, this was what she wanted, right? To know the events that had led him to this state.

"The villagers ... they thought I was a monster. And there was a child...."

A myriad of emotions went through her as he continued the story. Pity and sadness for the poor, dead boy. Some sympathy for the parents who, in the misplaced expression of their grief, sought a boogeyman they could blame for their terrible loss. And then, fury toward the men who hunted *her mate* without so much as giving him a chance to explain or showing him compassion. By the time he was done telling her, tears were pouring down her cheeks.

"Don't cry," he whispered. "Please ... not for me ..."

"Don't cry?" she said, her voice trembling with barely contained rage. "How could I not cry for you? Those men ... just because they weren't soldiers you might think they were innocent, but so were *you*. What were you supposed to do? Wait for them to kill you first? It was self-defense."

"They were just misguided and misinformed."

"And so, you've been keeping yourself prisoner up here, thinking that's the only way to atone for their deaths? Shutting yourself away from the world—from your mate—because of some misconceived notion of who's innocent and who's not? And if you ask me, you've already paid for your sins." She cupped his strong jaw in her palms. "Can't you see? How many people you've saved—me, Anna Victoria, Temperance, Daniel, Darcey, not to mention every lost hiker or shifter up here? I think your ledger's balanced by now. And it's time to forgive yourself."

In that moment, something changed in him. It was so subtle, yet fundamental, that she could feel the tectonic shift as if it was happening inside her too. "I love you, Krieger. I love everything about you. And yes, you're enough. You've always been enough."

Her fox yipped and barked with an emotion she hadn't felt from it in such a long time that it took her a moment to recognize it: pure, unadulterated happiness.

Mine, her fox shouted in joy. *Mine, mine, mine.*

He must have sensed it too because his eyes widened, and he leapt forward, pulling her into his arms.

Mine, his bear replied. *Mine, mine, mine.*

Then he captured her mouth in a kiss. A heat sizzled inside her, making her skin run warm and cold at the same time. Electric sparks burst inside her, emanating from her chest and moving out to spread all over her body. The kiss continued on and on, lips melding and caressing, tasting and savoring the feeling of being one with their mate. The mating bond formed, fusing their souls into one.

When they finally pulled away for air and she opened her eyes, another tectonic shift occurred.

There it was. The indescribable blue that could make the sky jealous.

"John." Her voice trembled. "H-have I ever told you that your eyes ... they're so beautiful. I've never seen anything as blue as them."

He gaped at her. "Dutchy ... are you ... can you ..."

She nodded. "Yes." It was overwhelming, all the colors she could see, filling her synapses with information to process. The shades of brown of the cabin's walls. The hunter green blanket on top of the bed. The riotous array of the book spines lining the shelves. But none of that compared to the sight she'd been longing to see the most. "I love you," she said, beholding his blue eyes.

He lifted her up into his arms and carried her to bed. "I love you, too, Dutchy."

———

The sun wasn't even out when Dutchy's eyes fluttered awake the next day. Krieger was curled up behind her, arms surrounding her, the delicious warmth from his body reminding her of the hours they spent making love. She could stay like this forever.

Yet, she had an urge to get up. To do ... something.

He barely stirred when she pried his arms off. Still, it was a feat because they were as heavy as steel. Slipping out of bed, she put on his flannel shirt, then glanced around ... looking for ... *Ah! There.* She spotted the yellow legal pad by the CB radio. The top page had various scrawls on it—weather reports, schedules, and a bunch of acronyms and numbers she didn't recognize. She picked up the pad and the pen from the table, then headed out onto the porch.

Early dawn dominated the skies when she put pen to blank paper. Her hands moved swiftly, like they had a life of their own, drawing swirls and curves across the lines. By the time she stopped, the sun was peeking out from behind the mountains, painting the landscape with the dazzling blues, purples, and pinks of peak sunrise.

"What's that?"

She didn't start at Krieger's voice. No, she already knew he'd been behind her for a while now. Her hand and brain were just too focused on the task. "What do you think?" She held up the pad and turned to him.

He was leaning on the doorjamb, jeans over his hips but unbuttoned, arms crossed over his chest as his gorgeous blue eyes fixed on her. "Beautiful."

A blush covered her from head to toe. "I mean the dress." She stood up and thrust the yellow pad at him.

His brows wrinkled as he perused her sketch. "It's uh, a nice dress."

"It's for Temperance. Her wedding dress," she explained. "It just kind of came to me ... and I had to get it down." Temperance. She loved the name, and how it suited her nature. This dress too, with its trumpet silhouette and elegant lines, would show off the baker's natural beauty, allow *her* to shine. "Do you think she'll like it?"

He took a step forward and slipped his arms around her waist. "I think she'll love it," he said before his mouth descended on hers.

As she melted against him, her inner vixen, too, rejoiced. *Oh, you smart creature,* she said to her fox. It became clear to her now why it had hated him so. Krieger didn't break her. No, he broke her animal's trust. And, even when they had initially reconciled, it sensed that he wasn't ready for the mating bond. The sly little fox knew that he was still keeping something from them, something so important that would have made them both miserable if it continued to fester and prevent the bond from forming. The vixen didn't want only half of him—it wanted all of him, heart, mind, and soul—scars and all.

When he pulled away, he pressed his forehead to hers. "What are you thinking of, when you should only have one thing on your mind when I'm kissing you?"

She chuckled. "Make me breakfast and I'll tell you."

Epilogue

The Blackstone Rangers Headquarters' outdoor cafeteria hall was dressed to the nines in full fall regalia. Maple leaf-shaped streamers hung across the ceiling, crisscrossed with orange, red, and yellow fairy lights. Scarecrows were propped up in every corner, and pumpkins and gourds of all kinds, along with branches of maple leaves, sunflowers, and cornstalks were used as centerpieces on the tables that were pushed together to stretch across the room. A banner on the far wall greeted anyone who came in with Happy Thanksgiving.

Of course, the best feature of the place was the backdrop featuring the mountains. Though the leaves had mostly turned yellow and brown as the trees were preparing for the winter, it was still a stunning sight.

"Did you need more pine cones?" Dutchy asked Krieger as they sat at one of the tables, finishing the decorations. Beside them, Anna Victoria, Damon, Gabriel, and Temperance formed a kind of assembly line to finish up more decorative wreaths.

"Nah, all good," he said. His job was to glue the pine cones at the bottom of the wreath, a job that was mercifully idiot-proof because he had zero artistic talent.

"Thank you again for doing this, Dutchy," Damon said. He was at the end of the line, as he was assigned to put hooks on the backs of the wreaths. The Chief had even less artistic inclination than Krieger, if that were possible.

"You're welcome, Damon," Dutchy said. "Happy to do it."

Dutchy had volunteered to decorate the cafeteria for the Thanksgiving celebration. Actually, it wasn't the actual day, but the day before. However, it was tradition for the rangers to throw a Thanksgiving celebration for the employees and their families before everyone went off for the holiday. Krieger had never attended the party—nor had he been to any kind of holiday get-together in years. This year, though, he and Dutchy were flying out tonight on the red eye to Minnesota to spend the long weekend with his family.

His mother and grandmother had practically been in tears when he called home to tell everyone about Dutchy and that they'd be coming home for the holidays. Of course, when he asked if he could have the family ring as he was going to ask Dutchy to marry him when they got there, the two women cried buckets and promised to make sure the Krieger family heirloom would be ready and polished.

Nervous energy filled him now, thinking of when he would ask her. Should he do it tomorrow as soon as they woke up? Or during dinner? Should he wait until after, when Thanksgiving was over so their engagement wouldn't be upstaged by the biggest holiday of the year?

It was a problem he had yet to solve, and time was running out. He was determined to find the right time to propose, but when would that be?

"It looks like Thanksgiving came in here and threw up all over the place!" J.D.'s enthusiastic exclamation shook him out of his thoughts. "I *love* it! Thanks for inviting me." The cat—

rather, the African black-footed cat—shifter bounded toward them wearing her usual trucker hat, jeans, and a sweater with a picture of a roasted turkey on it that proclaimed, "I like Big Breasts and I Cannot Lie."

"J.D. loves the holidays," Damon said to everyone at the table. "In case none of you noticed."

"I do!" J.D. proclaimed as she plopped down beside Dutchy. "I love Halloween because that means it's almost time for Thanksgiving, and I love Thanksgiving because it means soon it'll be my favorite holiday of all time—Christmas! Woot!" She pumped her fist in the air.

"Oh God," Gabriel slapped a hand on his forehead. "I forgot what a nightmare you are during the holidays."

"I am not a nightmare," she denied.

Damon raised a brow. "Remember that time you dragged us to Verona Mills so you could see Santa Claus and then got us kicked out of the mall because you fought with Santa's elf?"

"That wasn't my fault," J.D. said. "He clearly lacked the Christmas spirit and needed to do a better job of representing the good elves of the North Pole."

"You called him out because he wouldn't let you sit on Santa's lap," Gabriel said.

"See?" She spread her arms wide, as if proving her point. "Lack of Christmas spirit."

"You were sixteen," Damon pointed out.

J.D. harrumphed. "Unlike the sign they posted outside the Christmas village, the lyrics of that famous song didn't say 'to kids from *only* one to twelve' now did it?" She stuck her tongue out at Damon and Gabriel, then turned to Dutchy and grabbed one of the rolls of ribbons on the table. "Can I help?"

"Sure," Dutchy said. "Here ... let me show you."

Krieger wasn't quite sure what happened—one moment,

Dutchy was showing J.D. how to make bows for the wreaths and the next, the mechanic had unrolled the entire spool, the red and gold ribbon was tied up in knots, and she had somehow cut her fingers in three places.

"Uh, so did I do it right?" she asked Dutchy sheepishly, holding up a monstrosity of a wreath.

"J.D.!" Dutchy exclaimed. "What did you—how did you even manage to get these maple leaves wrapped up in here?"

"What?" J.D. asked innocently. "I thought it looked festive!"

"Happy Thanksgiving!" Daniel greeted as he walked up to them, Sarah in tow. Sarah and Darcey's younger brother, Adam, followed behind them in his motorized wheelchair. "Wow, this looks amazing, Dutchy," the bear shifter said.

"Yeah, the decorations are stunning," Sarah raved.

"Hey," Adam greeted, chin lifting in that 'I'm too cool to say Happy Thanksgiving' kind of way only a teenager could pull off. "What's up? When do we eat? I'm starving."

"Starving already?" Anders groaned as he strode up to them, Darcey by his side. "You just ate three slices of pizza at home." He shook his head exasperatingly. "But, great job, Dutchy," he said, then grimaced when he looked at J.D.'s wreath. "Now *that* looks like your handiwork, McNamara."

"Go fuck a French horn, Stevens," she hissed.

"Be a nice kitty now," he chortled. "So ... how about caracal?"

J.D. crossed her arms over her chest. "Nuh-uh, you're not going to make me say it."

Anders had found out that J.D. had shifted in front of Dutchy and Krieger, and had begged them to tell him what J.D. was. They refused, of course, and now he was a man on a mission, trying to discover her animal. He took a guess each time they crossed paths, but had yet to get it right.

Darcey rolled her eyes. "I apologize for my mate. I swear I can't take him anywhere."

"It's all right, Darcey. Don't apologize for him." Getting to her feet, J.D. turned to Anders. "However, I think *you* owe an apology to a tree somewhere for providing you oxygen."

"Hey!" Anders protested.

J.D. chuckled. "All right, I'm gonna go look for some snacks. I'll see you guys around." With a wave of her hand, she walked off in the direction of the entrance to the main building.

"You know," Darcey said. "It's not just her animal that's the mystery here."

"Really?" Anders asked. "What else could it be?"

The swan shifter's brows drew together. "Does anyone know what 'J.D.' stands for?"

Everyone looked at each other, puzzled.

"Gabriel?" Temperance asked her fiancé.

"What're you looking at me for?" The lion shifter raised his palms up. "Do I look like I'd know?"

"Not even you, Damon?" Anna Victoria asked, astonished.

"Er. Uh." The chief scratched his head. "We've been friends for so long, at this point, I'm too afraid to ask."

As they continued with their wreath making, more people poured into the cafeteria hall. The din began to grow louder, and at one point, Dutchy reached out and placed a hand over his. "Are you okay?" she asked.

The warmth of the pale blue eyes filled with concern was almost enough to chase away the anxiety building in him. While he wanted to reassure his mate that he was perfectly fine, he didn't want to lie to her. Actually, he couldn't, because surely, she could tell his unease through their mating bond. "I need some air."

"You go ahead," she said. "I'll finish up and join you in a bit, okay?"

"Thanks." He got up and left without a word. No one at the table questioned him or asked him where he was going or why he was leaving—after all, after Dutchy, these were the men who understood him the most.

Shoving his hands into his pockets, he strolled outside toward the edge of the parking lot where he could see Contessa Peak in the distance. It was early yet, but with the days growing shorter, he knew the sun would descend behind the peak soon. He stood there, enjoying the silence and being alone, at least, until he felt a presence behind him.

"It is a beautiful sight," Milos said as he stepped up beside Krieger.

"Sure is." No, he wasn't startled by the wolf shifter's presence. What did catch him by surprise was the fact that Milos was dressed casually in jeans, boots, a T-shirt, and wool coat. He also wore a black patch over his scarred eye and had a duffel bag slung over his shoulder. "You leaving?"

He nodded. "There are things back home on Lykos I must attend to."

"D'you gotta go right now?" Krieger cocked his head back toward the hall. "Caterers should be by with the food soon. Why don't you stay for a bite?"

"I'm afraid I cannot. Petros is coming to pick me up to take me to the airport. But before that, I shall be dining with his family. I cannot leave without seeing my little Sofie." The corner of his lips tugged up in the closest thing Krieger had seen to any emotion from the Greek wolf. "But I came here to give you some news. About the poachers and their victims."

Krieger didn't know this until Petros Thalassa had told him, but Milos had been part of the original Shifter Protection Agency back on the island of Lykos under their Alpha, Ari Stavros. He'd been injured during a mission and was thought to be dead, but their enemies actually captured and tortured him, which was what had sent him into a downward spiral.

"Petros tells me they have tracked down all the missing shifters," Milos said. "They are in the process of repatriating all three."

"H-how are they?" His teeth clenched, thinking about what those poor shifters might have gone through.

"Alive," was all Milos said. "And as for the people responsible for their kidnapping, they have also been found and will soon be brought to justice."

"Tell Petros if they need help ..."

Milos nodded. "I shall pass the message along."

"I should get back." Krieger stuck his hand out. "Good luck to you, Milos." It was hard to believe that Milos would be leaving, but he hoped this wasn't goodbye forever.

Milos grabbed it and squeezed. "Same to you, my friend."

"Sure I can't convince you to come in for at least a beer?"

The wolf shifter turned to the mountains. "Thank you, but no. I should like some time to myself before Petros arrives."

Krieger understood, not offended by the rebuff or the dismissal. "Sure thing, bud."

Turning on his heel, he left the wolf shifter and headed back to the cafeteria. Even more people had come in now, but the fresh air outside had calmed his bear enough that he could walk in without any problem.

What his bear *did* complain about was that they had been away from their mate. So, he sought her out, finally finding her fixing the hat on one of the decorative scarecrows by the refreshment tables.

Sidling up behind her, he placed his hands on her waist. She barely reacted, though he could feel her vixen yipping in happiness. His bear, too, replied with a growl of pleasure.

"So," he said, leaning down to her ear. "I leave you alone for five minutes, and you're already messing around with another guy."

Turning on her heel, she raised a brow at him. "At least this guy doesn't try to feel me up every chance he gets."

"You like it when I feel you up." To prove a point, he moved his hand lower, down to her luscious ass and squeezed. "Hmmm ... I can't wait to get you alone tonight."

She pressed up against him, then slipped her hand over the bulge now growing in his crotch. "Why wait?"

"Oh, you're in trouble, missy."

She stifled a laugh as he grabbed her hand and tugged her toward the door that led into the main building of the Blackstone Ranger's headquarters. As soon as they were alone, he caught her mouth in a kiss and pressed her up against the wall. She melted into him, molding her sweet body against his and rubbing against him until he could smell her arousal. "Krieger," she moaned. "What if someone comes in?"

He growled, but pulled away from her. He needed to be alone with her. Now. "C'mon." He put a hand around her shoulder.

"Where are we going?" she asked as they shuffled along the darkened hallway.

"I know a place we can be alone."

"Where?"

He grinned at her. "Damon's office."

"Dam—oh!" Her blue eyes sparkled. "Lead the way then."

The chief's office was the perfect place for a secret rendezvous as it was located on the far end of the building and had a great view of the mountains. The thought of bending her over that big desk was enough to make his cock twitch painfully.

When they got to the door at the end of the hall, he

hurriedly pushed her inside, his arousal in such full force that he didn't realize the office wasn't empty.

Lusty shrieks, moans and grunts greeted them as they stumbled inside, as well as two very naked figures currently using the desk as their own personal sex furniture.

Dutchy's face was that of pure horror. "Not again!"

"Fuck!" He didn't expect Damon and Anna Victoria would have the same idea as them. *Goddamned Damon has this office every other fucking day of the year, and he had to feel frisky* now?

The pants and groans, however, didn't sound like the chief and his wife. His vision focused on the copulating couple on the desk. Though he couldn't see the man's face, the woman's was turned to them. Krieger's brain once again short-circuited when he recognized who it was.

J.D.'s light hazel eyes snapped open. "Oh my God!" she shrieked when she saw them.

Both of them stood still, unable to move. To his credit, J.D.'s partner didn't seem to mind the audience as he continued on.

"You're still here?" she exclaimed between the vigorous thrusting. "Were you raised in a barn? Get out!" Something sailed their way—a stapler probably—and he had to stand in front of Dutchy so it hit him in the chest instead of her.

"Sorry!" Dutchy waved, then grabbed him by the waist and pulled them both away. The door closed loudly behind them, though the faint sounds of the passionate couple were still audible to their shifter ears. "Oh my God, was that really ... did we really ..."

"I don't want to talk about it," he said with a grimace. He wondered how many beers he'd need to erase this particular memory. "C'mon, I know a better place."

Krieger found the staircase up to the second floor of the building, then the doorway that led to a spiral staircase that led up to the rooftop. "Careful," he said, then took her hand to guide her across. On this side of the building, they had a clear view of the skies over the mountains where twilight was slowly creeping in from the distance.

"How did you know about this place?" she asked.

"Well," he scratched his head. "Damon, Gabriel, Daniel, Anders, and me used to sneak up here to drink and hang out past curfew." Since he didn't like going into town on their days off from training, the guys didn't want him to feel left out, so they would sneak him in some beer, and they would come up here to drink and talk and shoot the shit. Well, *they* did anyway. He was happy to sit back and listen as he watched the stars.

"It's lovely here." She let out a little shiver, and so he sidled up behind her and wrapped his arms around her.

"Better?"

"Mm-hmm," she said, leaning into him.

They stood there for what seemed like the longest time, watching the day turn into night, the dark-blue sky glittering with stars.

His bear rumbled with real happiness, something he hadn't felt in a long time. Change didn't happen overnight. He still had a lot of work to do on himself. But in this moment, feeling Dutchy's love and trust through their mate bond, he knew he could continue on this journey without fear or doubt.

Spinning her around, he kissed her soundly on the lips, pushing his own emotions of love into the bond back to her. His heart thudded in his chest and then a thought came into his head. *This was it. The right time.*

"What are you thinking of?" she asked saucily when she pulled away. "When you should be thinking of only one thing when you're kissing me?"

"I'm thinking that I love you," he said. "And I don't want to wait any longer."

"For what?"

Getting down on one knee, he took her hand in his, making her gasp. "I was trying to find the best time to do this. But, well … the best time was after that snowstorm, but I can't change what happened in the past. However, the second-best time is now."

Her eyes glittered with tears. "John …"

"I have the ring waiting for you back in Minnesota. Mom and Grandma will be disappointed I'm doing this without them, but maybe we can stage something to keep them happy."

She chuckled through her tears and nodded.

"So … Duchess Marie Forrester … can I be your husband?"

"John … oh, John, yes!"

He whooped and stood up, then hoisted her up into his arms. "I love you, mate." Soon to be wife.

"I love you too."

They stayed there for a while longer, enjoying the peace and silence, only the sounds of the Thanksgiving party in full swing below them drifting up to where they stood, entwined in each other's arms, and the stars twinkling overhead as they watched from the heavens.

———

If you want to read a hot, sexy bonus scene from this book just join my newsletter here

http://aliciamontgomeryauthor.com/mailing-list/

You'll get access to ALL the bonus materials from all my books and my **FREE** novella **The Last Blackstone Dragon.**

But the story's not done yet!

Want to know who J.D. was caught with?

Find out by reading the next book

Blackstone Ranger Scrooge

Available at selected online bookstores.

Turn the page for a special preview.

Sneak Peek: Blackstone Ranger
Scrooge
RELEASES HOLIDAY 2020

"Motherfucking ball sack!" J.D. McNamara cursed as a big glob oil hit her on the cheek. Of course, oil, dirt, and grime were all part of being a mechanic and working with cars. But still, it was annoying as fuck. Her inner animal too, didn't like it. The feline sniffed at her distastefully, whipping its short tail around.

Damn prissy little thing.

Her inner feline yowled in protest.

Oh, J.D. knew her animal was fierce. It was dubbed as the deadliest cat in the world after all. But its small stature didn't exactly do them any favors, especially when compared to the other shifters in town.

While the population of Blackstone, Colorado was made up of a variety of shifter animals, most were inevitably predators like bears, large cats, and wolves. However, she was none of those. In fact, she was a very rare shifter—an African black-footed cat, one of the smallest wildcats in the world. Few people knew who she was because ... well, it was hard to explain it exactly and inevitable people would just think she was just a cat.

"You all right there, J.D.?" came a familiar voice from above.

Finishing up the repair, she slid out from under the Toyota she'd been working on and looked up at Gabriel Russel's grinning face. "Yeah, yeah," she sighed.

"You didn't sound like you were all right," he teased, but offered her a hand.

She took it and allowed him to pull her up. "Yeah, well next time why don't you get a money shot on the fucking face, Russel and see if you like it."

"I'd tell you to act like a lady, but you'd probably knee me in the balls," he chuckled.

"Damn right." She grabbed a rag and wiped the oil from her face. "Besides, people who cuss are smart as fuck. It's scientific fact." She threw the dirty rag at him playfully, but he blocked it with a hand.

"Whoah, watch the hair!" He shook his head, making his long, dark golden locks shimmer. It was almost comical and very apt—Gabriel was a lion shifter, after all, and was as proud of his human mane as he was of his animal's. "Just because you don't care about what you look like, doesn't mean some of us don't."

"Some meaning *you*." Taking her trucker cap off the hook from the wall, she placed it on top of her head. It was the only way she could cover her mop of unruly blonde curls. If she spent time on trying to tame it every morning to have it perfect the way Gabriel did, she'd have to wake up at five everyday. "So, to what do I owe this pleasure, Russel?" Not that Gabriel needed an occasion to show up at her garage. They had been best friends since grade school after all.

"Oh yeah." He held up his hand, lifting up a white box. "Temperance wanted you to have this. Ginger pumpkin streusel pie. Her first Thanksgiving creation."

"Oooh!" Taking the box from him, she took in a sniff. The

smell of ginger, pumpkin, and spices tickled her nose. "I'm honored, but what's it for?"

"For not charging her for the tune-up and oil change," he said.

"Of course. You know what Pop always said. Family—"

"Don't pay," Gabriel finished with a fond smile on his face. "It means a lot to me. That you consider her family too."

"Like I wouldn't. She's your mate and soon-to-be-wife, so of course she's family. Besides, anyone who can put up with you deserves more than free service," she said with a chuckle.

"Oh ha ha, funny, McNamara, you should go on tour." Gabriel rolled his eyes. "Anyway, there's another reason I came here. Damon asked me to invite you to the Blackstone Ranger Thanksgiving party tomorrow."

"He did?" J.D. blinked. Damon was their other best friend, who was also chief of the Blackstone Rangers. Gabriel had been a ranger himself the past five years, but recently he quit so he could go into business with his mate to take over the local pie shop, Rosie's Bakery and Cafe. "I've never been asked before. I thought it was an event for rangers and their families?"

"Yeah, well, you're family, J.D.," Gabriel declared with a warm smile.

She stared at him, stunned, her throat closing up at the declaration.

Gabriel and Damon had been her best friends since she was ten years old, when she and her father had moved to Blackstone from Brooklyn. She'd been the new girl in town, which already made her a target for bullies but the fact that she was a tomboy didn't make it easier. But the two had stuck by her and protected her from mean girls who made fun of her for being a grease monkey's daughter. Yes, the three of them had always been tight, and they'd been with her through thick and thin, but well ... none of them were the sentimental type.

"J.D.?" Gabriel asked, the corner of his mouth turning up. "Are you crying?"

"Fuck no. It's all the dust in here." She turned around and sniffed. "Don't ya have to be somewhere else? Like counting the gold bars in your trust fund or something."

Gabriel laughed. "All right, all right. So, I'll see you tomorrow? We're all helping out Dutchy with the decorations and Temperance is bringing the desserts, so we'll be there early. Feel free to show up anytime but we eat at five."

"Sure." She turned her head and flashed him a smile. "See you tomorrow. Tell Temperance I said thank you for the pie."

"Will do." The lion shifter waved goodbye and strolled out of the garage.

After cleaning up her tools and calling one of her mechanics to move the Toyota, she headed out to the trailer/office out in the main garage lot.

"Hey Pop," she greeted the photo that hung up behind the desk inside the office. Jimmy McNamara smiled down at her as it always did, frozen in time. He'd been too young when he died in that accident, barely fifty. Shifters couldn't get most illnesses and they healed fast, but that truck that struck him down as he was crossing the street killed him on impact. His death had been a shock, and even now, a decade later, she still felt his loss so keenly. Even though she had taken over the business, this office was like a shrine to him—pictures of her as a kid and her mother, old school road signs, a black-and-white photo of the Brooklyn bridge, a classic James Dean photo of him on a motorcycle, and a framed and signed Billy Joel poster hung up on the walls.

Sitting down behind the desk, she went to work, checking her emails, inventory, and her accounting software. Finally, after what seemed like hours, she was done and she closed the laptop with a satisfying *click*.

"Whew!" Stretching her arms over her head, she leaned

back on the worn leather office chair. This was not her favorite part of owning J.D.'s Garage, but it had to be done. "Yikes!" She winced as she saw it was already dark outside. It was the Monday before Thanksgiving so while they were busy trying to get all the repairs done before the holidays. *But at least I'll have the long weekend to look forward to.* Grabbing her jacket from the back of the chair and the keys to her truck, she headed out the door.

"Hey J.D."

The unfortunately familiar voice made her freeze before she managed to finish locking the door to the office. With a deep breath, she turned around. "Hey Roy," she greeted back, pasting a smile on her face. "It's pretty late. What are you doing here?"

Roy Jorrell grinned at her sheepishly. "Well ... I'm having trouble with my car."

She crossed her arms over her chest. "Again?"

He nodded. "Yeah. There's this *clunk clunk clunk* sound whenever I start it up."

"It's late and I should be getting home. Maybe you can come back after the holidays?"

"But what if there's something wrong and I get stuck at home? Or on the side of the road?" He flashed her a boyish smile, his blue eyes twinkling. "Please, J.D.? You're the best mechanic in town."

Pop always said that you should never turn away business and to always treat customers well, but he was trying her patience. This was the third time this month he was back for some phantom sound or strange malfunction in his jacked-up GMC Sierra, but whenever she or one of her guys looked into it, his truck turned out to be perfectly fine. Why he kept coming back, she didn't know.

"Oh, all right," she said, resigned. "Let's go take a look."

She followed him to where he parked just outside the

garage. "Go and start the car and I'll check under the hood," she instructed him.

Minutes later, it was just as she thought—his truck was perfectly fine. "Nothing's wrong here," she said to him as she shut the hood.

"Oh?" He was suddenly behind her, startling even her own cat-like reflexes. "I could have sworn I heard something," he said, rubbing the back of his head with his palm.

"Uh-huh."

"So you got plans for the holidays?"

She turned around. "Yeah, I do."

"I'll probably just be alone," he said. "I didn't want to make the trip back to my folks in Florida since I was planning to see them for Christmas."

"Uh-huh," she said, trying to feign interest. "Well I should—"

"I was wondering if you wanted to have dinner with me."

"Excuse me?" She stared at him, hands on her hips. Roy had been a classmate back in high school, but he moved away sophomore year. He was some kind of avian shifter, if she recalled; he was mostly a loner at school, an emo kid who dressed in all black. But, like most people, he grew out of that phase and was some kind of computer programmer or something who worked from home. She ran into him at the diner last month, as he had recently moved back into town. That was when he started coming into the garage. *Is that why he'd been wasting her time?* Irritation grew in her, and her cat hissed, not liking this male one bit.

He swallowed. "I ... uh ... I mean, just to thank you. For being so patient with me."

J.D. thought about it for a moment. Roy was cute, she supposed, and he had a job and a full head of hair. What else did she want for in a guy? She'd been dating actively for almost twelve years now and he was a catch compared to all the losers she'd been with.

"J.D.?" Roy asked. "So? What do you think?"

"I think ... I think it's getting late." She sidestepped him.

"But what about that dinner?"

"I'll think about it, okay?" With a wave of her hand, she scampered to her truck. Shutting the door, she waited, watching Roy's truck as it drove away, then breathed a sigh of relief.

Why didn't I just say yes? She leaned her forehead down the steering wheel. Maybe it was turning thirty or seeing her best friends with their mates, but she was starting to get picky about who she went out with. Her last date had been months ago with an accountant she met on a dating app, it was *meh*. And the last guy she had the serious hots for? Well, he didn't even give her a second look. Besides, she was happy with her work, her life, and her social circle.

But now, all her friends had mates, including her last female friend, Dutchy Forrester, and she was starting to feel left out.

Sticking her key in the ignition, she started her car. Was she that oblivious that she missed the signs that he'd been coming to the garage to see her? That was it, right?

Maybe I should give Roy a chance.

Her cat hissed again.

"Oh, all right." Putting the truck into gear, she left the parking lot and headed home.

————

By the next day, J.D. had forgotten about the Roy thing and feeling sorry for herself for being alone. There were worse things than not having a boyfriend after all.

Besides there was no reason to be glum—not these days anyways. The holidays were her favorite time of the year. She remembered how magical it was growing up. The cool weather, the food, the infectious cheer. Who could be sad during Christmas, for crying out loud?

The days leading up to Christmas always sent her into a holiday high and she was pretty stoked for tonight's party. In the past, she and father celebrated Thanksgiving with Damon and his parents. Gabriel usually had to attend some kind of family dinner at the Russel estate, but he always managed to sneak off before dessert and join them. It was a tradition they continued, even after Pop passed and Damon was deployed and came back after being discharged. His parents had retired to Florida a couple of years back, but the three of them still got together on Thanksgiving. None of them could cook, unfortunately, so they would order Chinese takeout and watch football before her *favorite* tradition of all later that night.

Of course, this year was going to be a little different with the addition of the two more people—Damon's mate Anna Victoria and Temperance—but her best friends had assured her nothing would change.

And while she'd never been invited to the Blackstone Rangers Thanksgiving party before, she'd heard some stories about how amazing the spread was—turkey, mashed potatoes, sweet potatoes, cranberry sauce, green beans, corn, dinner rolls. *Hmmm.* Her mouth was watering, just thinking about it. This morning, she made sure to put on her best Thanksgiving sweater—the one with a roasted turkey on the front that proclaimed, "I like Big Breasts and I Cannot Lie." It was a big hit with the guys at the garage, so she was sure everyone at the party would love it.

After clocking out early for the day, she said goodbye to the crew and hopped into her truck. Since the rangers were in charge of keeping the mountains safe, their headquarters were located up in the Blackstone Mountains.

With the change in seasons, the trees and mountains presented a gorgeous view, making the drive a pleasant one, so she took her time. Eventually, she pulled up to the huge stone and log building stood at the entrance to the public area of the mountains and parked her truck in the nearest empty spot. The party was probably going to me in the big cafeteria in the back, so she circled around the main building and walked into the open-air hall. Sure enough, the place was fully dressed to the nines in fall colors and decorations.

"It looks like Thanksgiving came in here and threw up all over the place!" she exclaimed, her eyes taking in all the fall harvest decorations. "I *love* it! Thanks for inviting me."

Damon rolled his eyes when his saw her sweater. "J.D. loves the holidays, in case none of you noticed."

"I do!" Seeing the empty spot next to Dutchy Forrester, she plopped down beside the fox shifter. "I mean, I love Halloween because that means it's almost time for Thanksgiving and I love Thanksgiving because it means soon it'll be my favorite holiday of all time—Christmas! Woot!" She pumped her first in the air.

"Oh God," Gabriel slapped a hand on his forehead. "I forgot what a nightmare you are during during the holidays."

"I am *not* a nightmare," she denied.

Damon raised a brow. "Remember that time you dragged us to Verona Mills so you could see Santa Claus and then got us kicked out at the mall because you fought with Santa's elf?"

Oh yeah. How could she forget? As far as she knew, she was still banned from entering Valley Fair Mall. "That wasn't my fault," J.D. said. "He clearly lacked the Christmas spirit and needed to do a better job of representing the good elves of the North Pole."

"You called him out because he wouldn't let you sit on Santa's lap," Gabriel said.

ALICIA MONTGOMERY

"See?" She spread her arms wide, as if proving her point. "Lack of Christmas spirit."

"You were sixteen," Damon pointed out.

J.D. harrumphed. "Unlike the sign they posted outside the Christmas village, the lyrics of that famous song didn't say 'to kids from ONLY one to twelve', now did it?" She stuck her tongue out at Damon and Gabriel, then turned to Dutchy, grabbing one of the rolls of ribbons on the table. "Can I help?"

"Sure," Dutchy said. "Here ... let me show you."

Her friend patiently showed her how to tie the shiny gold and red ribbon into bows. *Hmmm, simple enough*, she thought. However there was something missing with the wreathes. They didn't look festive enough. So, she decided to unroll the entire spool so she could make bigger and better ribbons. Glancing around, she found a bunch of what looked like leftover decor stuff under the table.

Oooh! She grabbed a handful of maple leaves, some pine cones, an ear of corn, and a mini pumpkin. It took a lot of work —not to mention cuts on her fingers, but she somehow managed to get everything on an empty wreathe.

"Uh, so did I do it right?" she asked Dutchy sheepishly as she held up her creation.

"J.D.!" Dutchy exclaimed. "What did you—how did you even manage to get these maple leaves wrapped up in here?"

"What?" J.D. asked innocently. "I thought it looked festive."

"Er, it's certainly ... interesting," Dutchy said. "But ... let me give you some tips ..."

As Dutchy helped her put her wreath to rights, more people joined them, including Daniel Rogers, his mate Sarah and her adopted brother Adam. Of course, where they went, Darcey Wednesday, Sarah's sister came too, along with her mate, Anders Stevens.

" ... but, great job, Dutchy," Anders said. When his gaze

landed on J.D.'s wreathe, he grimaced. "Now *that* looks like your handiwork, McNamara."

"Go fuck a French horn, Stevens," she hissed.

"Be a nice kitty now," he chortled. "So ... how about caracal?"

J.D. crossed her arms over her chest. "Nuh-uh, you're not going to make me say it." The tiger shifter had been impossible ever since he found out she had shifted in front of other people and was not trying to guess what she was. Well, he would never find out, not if she could help it.

Darcey rolled her eyes. "I apologize for my mate. I swear I can't take him anywhere."

"It's all right, Darcey. Don't apologize for him." Getting to her feet, she turned to Anders. "However, I think *you* owe an apology to a tree somewhere for providing you oxygen."

"Hey!" Anders protested.

J.D. chuckled. "All right, I'm gonna go look for some snacks." She had forgotten to eat lunch since she was rushing to get all her work done and now her stomach was gurgling with hunger. "I'll see you guys around."

Getting up from the table, she made her way into the main building. There was a vending machine somewhere on the first floor, but couldn't quite remember where.

Since everyone was probably outside waiting for the festivities to begin, it was empty inside half the lights had been turned off. She walked down the main corridor, tapping her finger on her chin. *Maybe it was by the locker room. Or the observation deck downstairs? Or—wait.* An idea popped into her head.

Damon loved peanut butter cups and when she had lunch with Anna Victoria the other day, she had seen her with a big bag of them. When she asked who they were for, Anna Victoria said it was for Damon to keep in his desk so he would stop being such a grumpy bear when he was busy and forgot to eat lunch.

Heading down the darkened hallway, she made her way to the very end where the door to Damon's office was. She crept inside and dashed to the large oak desk, opening the bottom drawer on the right.

"Damon, you magnificent predictable bastard," she exclaimed when she saw the drawer overflowing with not only peanut butter cups, but also other candy. "Don't mind if I do," she cackled, ripping a packet of peanut butter cups and devouring both. Before closing the drawer, she stuffed her jeans pockets with more candy and chocolate. Satisfied with her haul, she zipped toward the door. As she prepared to shove her weight against it, however, the door swung open and J.D. found herself sailing forward.

"Shit!" Momentum kept her flying until she collided with something solid and hard. "What the—*oomph!*" She landed on the floor with a hard thud, the wind knocked out of her. It took her a second before realizing that it wasn't the floor she landed on. No, she was right on top of someone. A living, breathing someone, based on the rise and fall of the chest she was now plastered to. "I'm so—oohhh!" A delicious male scent teased her nostrils and she pressed her nose against the khaki fabric underneath her, taking a big whiff. *Hmmm.* That scent made her want to curl into a ball and wrap it around her herself. Strangely, her cat felt the exact same way. *Huh.* Her prickly little feline *never* had an opinion on any male ... ever.

"If you wouldn't mind ..."

The smooth voice sent tingles across her skin. "Actually, I do mind—hey!"

She found herself being pushed away, then hauled up to her feet as warm, callused hands gripped her arms. "What do you think you're doing, tossing me around like a sack of—" A gasp left her mouth as her gaze collided with the most unusual blue-violet eyes she'd ever seen. Even behind the gold-rimmed glasses, she could feel them examining her with a cold, detached curiosity.

Mine, her cat purred from out of nowhere.

And his animal let out a triumphant roar as it answered back: *Mine!*

"Well, fuck me sideways," J.D. breathed out. "You're—"

"My mate," he finished, that cool stare never leaving hers.

The low, edgy growl that rumbled from his chest sent heat straight to her nether regions. "Oooh," she moaned, her knees weakening. *Control yourself, woman,* she chided herself as she leaned back to steady herself on the door. *You too, you little hussy*, she told her cat, which was now laying down on the ground, rolling on its back and showing its belly. *Oh come on now. Play it cool.* That was the plan anyway, at least until she lifted her head to meet those eyes again.

The icy, unaffected gaze slowly melted as his blue-violet eyes ignited with desire. Before she knew it, he pushed her against door, his hands moving from her shoulders up to her neck and jaw as he lowered his head to hers.

Holy fucking moly.

His mouth attacked hers hungrily, like he'd been starving for weeks. Another growl sent her hormones through the roof. When she tried to move her hands up, he gripped her wrists and pinned them over her head.

Jesus Henry Christ, her panties practically flooded at the dominant move and she melted against him. His lips never left hers as he continued to devour her, their kisses rough and wild as they teeth and tongues clashed. At some point he had lifted her up and held her against the door, her legs wrapping around his waist. Finding her hands free, she wrapped her arms round his neck to bring him closer.

She rubbed her hips against him, enjoying the little thrills that shot up her spine as the friction hit just right against her clit through their clothes. His hands cupped her ass, bringing her forward onto the hard bulge growing in his pants.

"God ... need you ..." he groaned.

"Yes," she said as she reached under her, grabbing the handle and twisting it until the door swung open, his gait steady as he walked them back inside Damon's office. The loud thud of the door closing didn't even register in her brain as her body temperature rose and that need to be with him, to have him inside her, eclipsed every other thought in her brain.

Buy Blackstone Ranger Scrooge now!

Available at select online bookstores

About the Author

Alicia Montgomery has always dreamed of becoming a romance novel writer. She started writing down her stories in now long-forgotten diaries and notebooks, never thinking that her dream would come true. After taking the well-worn path to a stable career, she is now plunging into the world of self-publishing.

 facebook.com/aliciamontgomeryauthor

 twitter.com/amontromance

 bookbub.com/authors/alicia-montgomery